Also by Monica Hughes

THE OTHER PLACE

THE OTHER PLACE

MONICA HUGHES

HarperCollins*Publishers*Ltd

http://www.harpercanada.com

HarperCollins books may be purchased for educational, business,
or sales promotional use. For information please write:
Special Markets Department, HarperCollins Canada,
55 Avenue Road, Suite 2900, Toronto,
Ontario, Canada M5R 3L2.

First edition

Canadian Cataloguing in Publication Data

Hughes, Monica, 1925–
The other place

ISBN 0-00-648176-0

I. Title

PS8565.U34083 1999   jC813'.54   C99-931145-X
PZ7.H83Ot 1999

00 01 02 03 04 HC 8 7 6 5 4 3

Printed and bound in the United States

THE OTHER PLACE

CHAPTER ONE

BANG! BANG! I woke up, sleepily wondering if the thunderous knocking on the door was part of a dream. Then it came again, even louder, and I thought, stupidly, *There aren't such things as burglars nowadays, but someone's trying to break down our apartment door.* I jumped out of bed and looked around for a weapon, but the only thing that met my sleepy eyes was a shoe. It had a pretty good heel on it, though, so with the shoe tightly grasped in my right hand, I opened the bedroom door and slipped out.

They were inside now, but they weren't burglars. On the contrary. Our small living room was packed with broad-shouldered men in black uniforms, the shoulder blaze of Earth's globe surrounded by an olive wreath proclaiming who they were. The World Government Police—WOGPO. This was *really* bad. The shoe slipped from my hand and clattered to the floor.

Mom was doing the talking. She's a high-powered lawyer who spends much of her time working on human-rights cases—there's a lot of money in them these days—and she was throwing precedents and procedures at the guy in front, the man in the good suit who was backed up by the broad-shoulders, with their narrow eyes and lips. Hadn't I seen him somewhere before?

Mom talked and talked while Dad just stood there, and the man from WOGPO shook his head once in a while. Finally she ran out of words, and he reached into the breast pocket of his uniform jacket and handed her a

1

folded piece of paper. Mom unfolded the paper and read it, and I could see her face turn white, as if all the blood had been sucked right out of it. She stood staring at it as if she'd been turned into an ice statue until the man leaned forward and plucked the paper from her hand.

Only then did she unfreeze. "But you c-can't . . ." she stammered. "It's . . . it's totally unconstitutional."

He shook his head. "I warned you and your husband, ma'am. Two days ago."

Then I remembered. He had come to the apartment late one evening and talked softly. After he had left, Mom and Dad had quarrelled, and I had gone into Gordie's room to sit with him until the angry voices had quietened.

Now the man was still shaking his head. "I can enforce this. And I must. It's the law. You're out of date, ma'am."

"But I've done nothing subversive. As for Alison and Gordie—" She gestured towards me, and I turned and saw that Gordie had crept out of his bedroom and was lurking just behind me. "You can see that they're only children. They've done nothing . . ."

Her voice faded as he continued to shake his head. He had a kind face and a gentle manner. If the heavies had not been there, filling the living room with their menace, I could have pictured us asking him to sit down, to have a cup of coffee.

Mom turned on Dad. "Doug, *do* something. Tell them I'm not responsible for those articles. *I* didn't write them, *you* did. I warned you to be careful, but you wouldn't listen, oh no, not you. You've got this image of yourself as some ancient hero, going off to conquer dragons. Now look where your foolishness has got us."

Dad said nothing, but he stepped forward and held out his hands, wrists together, as if he were waiting to be handcuffed, the way criminals were back in the old days. He looked so noble, tears flooded my eyes. *My father: the righter of wrongs. The writer of wrongs. How brave you are!* I thought.

Then I found myself remembering something my friend Kristin had said. "Your dad doesn't take things seriously," she'd told me, her lip curling. "It's like he thinks he's an actor. He'll be sorry. You'll see."

Now Mom screamed at him, almost in Kristin's words. "Oh, stop play-acting, Doug. Can't you see this is serious?"

The man in charge echoed Mom. "No need for this display, sir. I know you'll submit quietly. As for your wife and children, you knew the risk you were taking when you posted those articles on the Worldnet attacking the Government. I warned you that we could no longer ignore them."

Dad laughed, a dry laugh with no humour in it. "I had hoped that enough brave people would respond and force an inquiry into the fate of the disappeareds."

"Disappeareds?" The man raised his eyebrows. "What disappeareds?" Without waiting for an answer he turned to Mom. "As for you, Mrs. Fairweather, your legal arguments are impressive, but have you forgotten 'guilt by association'? You are a family, a legal unit. You are all responsible for each other."

"Guilty of what?" I interrupted. "Dad, you haven't done anything wrong, have you? Tell them. Explain. Don't just *stand* there."

I stamped my foot and moved towards him. I wanted to shake him, make him defend himself—and us. But before I'd taken more than a step, the broad-shoulders also moved—not far, just a warning step towards me.

The man in charge ignored me completely. He unfolded the piece of paper again and read it aloud. "For crimes of subversion against World Government, you, Douglas John Fairweather, accompanied by your lawful spouse, Carolyn Wilson Fairweather, and your minor offspring, Alison and Gordie Fairweather, will be transported to a penal colony in another place, where you will serve your sentence of five years in isolation. Long live World Government." He folded the paper and returned it to his pocket before stepping back.

Dad spoke for the first time. "What about a trial?"

"You have already been tried."

"And sentenced?"

"As you can see."

"So what I wrote in those articles *is* true. You can hardly deny it now. Tried and sentenced for speaking freely, with no opportunity to defend myself?"

"Your articles were grossly biased, Mr. Fairweather."

"They were the truth."

"False truths. That is your crime, sir."

I don't know how long they might have gone on throwing words to and fro, but at this moment Gordie made a run for it. I can't think what was in his mind as he turned and bolted down the passage towards the bedrooms. Our apartment was on the thirty-fifth floor and the only exit was the front door.

He had taken only two or three steps when the heavies had their guns out.

"No!" I yelled, but they paid no attention. I turned and saw Gordie lying in an untidy heap on the floor, like a puppet with the strings cut. *My little brother!* Without stopping to think, I jumped at the men and a microsecond later felt my body go numb. My knees turned to jelly and then the floor came up and hit me.

You know the feeling just before you wake up properly? Warm and secure, relaxed, kind of floating, while all kinds of thoughts and waking dreams drift through your mind. Like pictures and sounds on a vidscreen. You watch and listen, but you don't really react to them. They just pass by.

My first thought was just a feeling, the pleasure of being warm and comfortably cocooned. Lazily I wondered why that should be important—the climate control in our apartment was always set at a comfortable level—but now I had a memory of being cold, colder than I had ever been in my whole life, as cold as if I had been frozen. And now I was warm again . . .

I snuggled into the warmth and let the pictures drift by until I was jolted into awareness by the memory of a distant voice: "You will be transported to a penal colony in another place, where you will serve your sentence of five years in isolation . . ."

Penal colony. The words were as clear as if someone had just spoken them aloud. I remembered a map on the classroom vidscreen, and our social studies teacher, Ms. MacKenzie, speaking: "From 1788 to 1852, people who were guilty of even petty crimes, such as stealing a loaf of bread, were transported to a penal colony in Australia. Many of them elected to stay on after their sentences were completed, and a thriving settlement arose. Descendants of some of those early convicts became cattle and sheep barons who owned vast tracts of land in the new colony."

"A loaf of bread?" someone in class had commented. "Why would anyone want to steal *bread*?"

"In those days, over three hundred years ago, two hundred years before the establishment of World Government, many people were hungry. At times thousands upon thousands actually starved to death. Can someone tell me why that no longer happens? . . . Alison?"

In my dream state I felt my lips move. Felt the words in my throat. "Because our World Government has abolished poverty."

"Very good, Alison."

But what about mental poverty? I found myself thinking, and wondered lazily who had put that idea into my head. Kristin? Dad? There was the memory of voices quarrelling. Many memories. The voices drifted across my consciousness.

Dad's. "What sort of life will our children have when every decision is made for them, Carolyn? Where no dissent is allowed?"

Mom's. "You are always exaggerating, Doug. Taking the extreme view. But it's all talk, isn't it? You'd never actually do anything to change the situation, would you?"

Dad, laughing sarcastically. "Would *you*? You earn a fat salary as a so-called human-rights lawyer, better than mine, I'll admit. But who pays that salary? The Government, of course. Your work is just to paint over the messy bits and make the Government look good."

"Don't you dare imply that my work's not worthwhile, Doug Fairweather."

And so it would go until I broke in with the timid suggestion that dinner was overdue; or perhaps I'd just go ahead and make it myself, putting on a cheerful face so Gordie wouldn't think the family was breaking apart or anything upsetting like that. Maybe I concentrated on Gordie too much, but he really was a sweet kid and eight years old seemed to me kind of young to have to face the nitty-gritty facts of family fights.

"You're just so naive, Alison." Kristin's voice. "You've got to live in the real world."

"But I do!" I remember exclaiming in one of our many arguments. I longed for Kristin to admire me, but our relationship seemed to work the other way round. I admired *her* for her spunky stand in class, for her questions, which always seemed to go deeper than those the rest of us asked, for her amazing ability to go her own way, apparently untouched by the kindly brainwashing to which the rest of us succumbed. Why she liked me I was never sure. In class I gave the answers the teachers expected, without question, and got good marks for it. Did this make me naive?

"What about the disappeareds?" she challenged me. "Your dad writes about them on the Worldnet. Where are these people? They've never been formally tried. They just—vanish."

As Kristin did, one day in early summer. When she stopped coming to school and her name was wiped from the school rolls, the whispers began. Her whole family was gone. *Disappeared*. Only it wasn't I who asked Ms. MacKenzie about Kristin and her family but one of the other kids.

"The disappeareds are an urban legend," she had replied smoothly, and had gone on to tell us a number of gruesome stories, each of which was authenticated, not by the teller, but by someone the teller knew or had met at an airport or the corner store. Stories supposed to be true, but verified only at one remove. "So you see there *are* no disappeareds," she had concluded, and it wasn't until I was walking home after school that day that I'd realized she had never answered the original question: what had happened to Kristin and her family?

"You're so naive, Alison." I could hear Kristin's voice as if she were actually walking beside me, and that voice gave me the courage to go over to her apartment to try to find out where she had gone. There was a different name on the mailbox. A strange woman opened the door. She looked at me blankly when I asked for Kristin. "You must have the number wrong," she told me firmly and shut the door in my face. I went to the phone company and checked the listing on its computer, but the name wasn't there any more. It was as if she and her whole family—her mother, father and small brother Bobbie—had been wiped off the face of the Earth. Had I imagined Kristin? I found myself wondering. But how could I have? She was my friend. An old saying drifted through my mind. *Out of sight, out of mind.* It seemed to happen so easily. And how long would people remember?

I wanted to talk to Dad and Mom about my worries. After all, if Kristin and her family could vanish, it might happen to anyone. Even to us. But when I got home they were both out and Gordie, who'd got home before me, was frantic. "Where were you, Ally? I *needed* you." So I had to help him with his homework and get dinner ready, and try not to be mad inside because Mom and Dad weren't around when I needed *them*.

And then somehow the questions got lost in daily routine. In any case, I told myself, remembering Ms.

MacKenzie's comforting words, *World Government knows best. Now there is no more crime. No more hunger.* I drifted warmly back into deeper sleep.

When I finally woke up properly and opened my eyes, I thought I must be in hospital. Above me was not the familiar bedroom ceiling that I had painted deep blue and pasted with stars back in my space-travel phase; later I wanted to change it, but repainting over that dark blue would have been such a pain that I put it off.

This ceiling was pure white, enormously high above my bed, but curving down to meet the floor at my feet and to the right. The room itself was an odd shape, a small segment of a circle. There was nothing in it but the bed and an arc of built-in cupboards. *Was* I in hospital? I felt perfectly well.

"You will be transported to a penal colony in another place to serve your sentence of five years in isolation." The words echoed in my head.

Prison. This must be it. I sat up abruptly and felt the white room spin dizzily around me. I swallowed and shut my eyes. When my insides had settled, I opened my eyes again and cautiously swung my legs to the floor. I looked down and realized that I was no longer wearing my familiar pyjamas, but overalls of a sickly green colour. Apart from the zipper down the front there was no ornamentation of any kind. I was wearing plain black slip-on shoes. Basic clothing. Prison clothing, of course. I could feel panic rising and swelling like a balloon inside me.

"Hullo. Anyone there? Guard?" My voice was a dry croak and I wasn't surprised that no one heard me. I ran my tongue around my lips, swollen and cracked. How long had I been left without food or water? I had to have water. Was this some kind of torture? If so, I knew I wouldn't be able to hold out bravely, like a hero in an old spy story. But what secrets had I to tell?

I got to my feet and staggered to the door, my knees as wobbly as if I'd been bedridden for months. There were no bars, but the door would be locked of course. After all, this was a prison. "Guard," I called again, and pounded with my fists. "I'm so thirsty!"

Nothing happened. I slumped against the door, and it unexpectedly slid sideways into the wall. I stumbled out, caught my balance and took a couple of cautious steps. *This* was a prison cell?

Ahead of me was a living area with a couple of sofas, upholstered with black synleather in stark contrast to the gleaming white floor. Beyond them, cut off by a partition, I glimpsed the corner of a table and a couple of chairs. Directly to my right was a passageway with sliding doors on either side. Above, the high white ceiling curved down to the perimeter walls. I stared, turning round and round until I finally made sense of it. I was in a dome. A white windowless dome. Alone.

No, not alone surely. Mom and Dad must be somewhere close by. I called their names. Pounded on the closed doors. One of them slid open and there was Gordie. His cheeks were flushed with sleep and his dark hair stood up in a quiff on top of his head. He looked like a lost baby bird. He too was wearing prison-green overalls.

"Oh, Gordie, you're all right!" I ran to him, wrapped my arms round him and hugged him hard, feeling the narrow wings of his shoulder blades against my hands, smelling the little boy smell of sleep on his compact body, remembering with a shudder the square-shoul-dered men and the guns. Gordie falling like a broken doll. "Oh, Gordie," I said again and held him even more tightly, promising myself that I'd never let anything bad happen to him again.

He wriggled out of my arms. "Ally, I'm thirsty," he croaked.

"Me too. Let's see if we can find someone to give us water."

I led the way down the corridor. The door to his bedroom was open, and I glimpsed a room like mine in every particular, except that it was at the opposite curve of the dome. The bed was on the near wall, and the stor-age space was at the far end of the room.

The door at the blind end of the passage opened onto a bewildering array of machinery, but the door between my room and Gordie's slid open to reveal another room, this one with two beds. There were Mom and Dad, also dressed in green overalls and both sound asleep. Across the passage was a bathroom. *Water.* I looked around for a glass and didn't find one.

"There must be a kitchen on the other side of this unit. Come on, Gordie, we'll soon find your water." And sure enough, when I turned the corner into the living room and walked past the two sofas, I could see a counter and cupboards, a sink and taps.

I opened a cupboard, found drinking glasses and held them under the tap. They filled automatically to the brim. The water was cool, with a clean, slightly metallic tang, unlike the chemical taste of city water. I held it in my mouth and let it trickle slowly down my throat, easing the raspy dryness. I licked my lips and let the wetness linger on them. Long before I had finished mine, Gordie was holding out his glass and demanding more. I held it under the tap, but this time nothing happened.

"Sorry, Gordie. It seems to be rationed. Maybe we can find someone to ask."

"But I'm still thirsty." He wasn't exactly whining, but he was close to it. I swallowed my impatience and told myself that if I were finding the whole situation scary at age sixteen, what must it be like at eight years old, waking up in a strange and spooky prison?

"Never mind," I said soothingly. "You can have the rest of mine. Only drink this one more slowly, okay? I don't know when you'll be allowed more."

As Gordie obediently sipped the rest of my precious glass of water, I looked around. Where were the guards? How did they communicate with us or we with them? I realized that I had explored the whole dome. There was nothing more. We were in a white hemisphere of plas-teel, with no windows, no skylights. No vidphone that I could see. And apparently no spy cameras or microphones, unless they were hidden in the light panels overhead. But there had to be a door leading to the rest of the complex: other cells, guards' quarters and so on.

There were no human sounds. I strained my ears and heard only the faint whisper of an air conditioner and something else—a continuous soft, gritty sound I couldn't place at all. What could it be? I prowled the perimeter of the living area and finally discovered another sliding door—white on white—that I had missed in my first glance around. The exit.

"Locked, of course," I said out loud. But it wasn't. *Funny kind of prison*, I thought again as the door slid open. "Come on, Gordie. Let's see what's outside."

Only we weren't outside. We were in a triangle-shaped room facing another door that was built into the outside curve of the dome. On the left wall hung four scarlet jumpsuits, hooded, with big sock-like feet attached and gloves dangling at the ends of the sleeves. Above them were four sets of goggles. Centred on the outer door was a large notice printed in red. I read it out loud for Gordie's benefit.

DO NOT ATTEMPT TO OPEN THIS OUTER DOOR UNTIL YOU HAVE REVIEWED THE INTRODUCTORY VIDDISK.

DO NOT OPEN THE OUTER DOOR UNTIL THE INNER DOOR TO THE HABITAT HAS BEEN CLOSED AND YOU HAVE DONNED THE APPROPRIATE PROTECTIVE SUIT AND GOGGLES.

AFTER EXITING ENSURE THAT THE DOOR IS CLOSED BEHIND YOU AND THAT YOU HAVE FASTENED THE SAFETY CABLE TO THE TOGGLE ON YOUR SUIT.

ON REENTERING CLOSE THE DOOR BEHIND YOU. PRESS THE BUTTON MARKED "VACUUM PUMP". REMOVE AND HANG UP YOUR SUIT AND GOGGLES. DO NOT OPEN THE INNER DOOR UNTIL THE PUMP HAS CEASED OPERATING.

FAILURE TO FOLLOW THESE STEPS
MAY RESULT IN CONTAMINATION OF
THE ENVIRONMENT, INJURY OR EVEN
DEATH. THE PRISON AUTHORITIES
WILL NOT BE HELD RESPONSIBLE FOR
FAILURE TO OBSERVE THE ABOVE
GUIDELINES.

"Come on, Ally. Let's explore." Gordie tugged at my sleeve.

"Are you nuts? Didn't you listen to what that notice said? We don't really know what's out there." My voice faded and my throat felt suddenly dry again. *What kind of place needs an airlock and protective clothing? Where are we?*

I swallowed and tried to talk normally. "We'll leave exploring till later, Gordie. Right now let's wake Mom and Dad and have a family council."

Though Gordie is only eight, he's a bright kid. He stared at me blankly. "Family council? When did we ever—?"

"When you were little we used to talk things out. It's only recently things have been kind of . . ." I searched for the right word.

"Tense?" suggested Gordie.

"You're too smart for your own good, Gordie Fairweather. Come on. Let's wake them up."

But by the time I'd closed the inner door, Mom and Dad had come into the living room and were looking around dazedly. I filled two glasses and handed them over. Luckily the tap seemed to be working again.

"Where are we? What is this place?" Mom ran her hands through her hair. "It doesn't *look* like a jail."

"But of course it is. Our home for the next five years, I suppose," Dad muttered. He put his hands over his face.

"*Five years!*" Mom almost screamed. "I warned you, Doug—"

Before the familiar argument had a chance to get going, I interrupted. "There's a viddisk we're supposed to watch. Only I haven't found it yet. Or the screen."

"The screen's over here, Ally. I wonder if they've got good games."

"This is a prison, son, not an amusement centre." Dad's voice was biting, and I could see Gordie's lip quiver. I put an arm around his shoulder and squeezed. "It'll be okay," I whispered, lying.

For how could it possibly be okay? We were in prison. For five years. In "another place". What other place? I wondered.

The vidscreen was large, about a hundred and fifty centimetres square, and we hadn't noticed it before because it was set into the end of the wall that formed the block containing the bathroom. The two sofas were conveniently placed with their backs to the airlock, facing the screen. Beneath the screen were two shelves of viddisks, flanked by speakers.

Maybe there will be entertainment disks, I thought. Something to pass the time. Five years. One thousand, eight hundred and twenty-five days. Plus one leap-year day. One thousand, eight hundred and twenty-six days.

Gordie wriggled out from under my arm and ran over to pull the top disk from the pile. "'Introduction to life in Habitat W'," he read aloud. "There's lots more in small letters." He handed it to me and I read the label.

"'Play this disk before attempting to leave the dome,

15

prepare food or touch any of the dome's recycling or environmental controls.' So here goes. All we ever wanted to know about Habitat W." I inserted the disk into the slot and sat on one of the sofas. "Come on, Gordie, settle down." I tried to keep the quaver out of my voice, to hide the fact that I was terrified, and I told myself that nothing on this disk could be any worse than the crazy thoughts going through my head.

Like, this was a brainwashing unit, and when we came out we would be zombies. Like, they'd wait till we calmed down and got used to life here and then they'd gas us to death. Like, Habitat W was an experimental hospital and we were the test animals. I shivered. That was the scariest.

No, I told myself firmly. *None of these things will happen. We're stuck together in this dome for five years. Well, tough. Maybe it'll be a great chance to go back to being the kind of family I remember from when I was little. After all*, I thought, trying to cheer myself up, *Mom won't have a law practice and Dad won't be writing news stories for the Worldnet any more. They'll have time for Gordie and me.* A small voice inside me, like a reminder of Kristin, said, *Oh, Alison, you're so naive.* But I pushed it to one side and put my arm around Gordie, determined to think positive thoughts.

CHAPTER TWO

There was blank blue, a streak of black across the screen, and then the image cleared to the icon of World Government, the icon I had last glimpsed on the shoulder flashes of the heavies who had invaded our apartment—yesterday? the day before?—and zapped us. The follow-up message—WELCOME TO HABITAT W CORRECTIONAL FACILITY—didn't exactly make me want to cheer. Welcome? How bizarre!

The vid showed a plan of Habitat W, with arrows and explanatory text. We were told that the storage units in the bedrooms contained bed linen and spare overalls, and I wondered whether the "prison green" I was wearing was the only colour, or if we had some choice. Cherry red would be less depressing.

Water was definitely rationed. The lavatory in the bathroom was an electronic self-composting unit that used no water, and the laundry unit was a waterless electrostatic cleaner. As for the showers, they were monitored to deliver a one-minute shower daily for each of us, with an extra three minutes every five days for shampooing.

I'd managed to be strong and brave up to that point, but somehow this was the last straw. "Five days!" I screamed and burst into tears. "I'll die. How can I possibly go without washing my hair every day?"

"I'll trade you, Ally," Gordie offered. "If I don't shower, you'll get two minutes a day."

"You'll shower, Gordie Fairweather," Mom said firmly.

17

End of discussion. Her attitude cheered me up. It would be really great having Mom take charge again. *Maybe it is going to work*, I thought, and pushed the idea of greasy hair out of my head.

In the third section the vid focused on the kitchen, showing us the contents of the cupboards. They were mostly filled with solid stacks of prepackaged food, each pack marked with the day, the meal and the individual who was supposed to consume it. So my first meal of this first day in prison was to be 1, 1, FC—Female Child, that was me.

"The menu is varied for your health and personal gratification and is repeated on a ten-day basis. Each meal has been planned for optimum nourishment without excess for a person of the given sex, weight and age. You are cautioned that you must consume your own meal rather than making exchanges within the family unit. Moreover, since there are no facilities for storing perishables, you are required to consume meals at the designated time."

"I won't eat broccoli," Gordie said firmly.

"I don't suppose you'll get the chance. These meals will be the same kind of synthesized processed junk the Government stores hand out, I expect," Dad said drily.

"Please try *not* to put Gordie off his food, Doug. I have enough trouble with him at the best of times," Mom snapped back.

"Shh, they're on to the next bit," I interrupted.

The vid showed the processor—a white unit, a bit like a microwave—that sat on the kitchen counter. All we had to do was insert the four trays for a particular meal, then the code would be read, and the food baked, steamed or otherwise reconstituted. Presto, a meal.

Eighteen hundred and twenty-six days, I remembered. Times twelve, for three meals a day for the four of us. "How can there possibly be room in these cupboards for twenty-one thousand, nine hundred and twelve food packages?" I asked after a bit of mental arithmetic. "Suppose we run out?"

"You may wonder how the kitchen is able to deliver food to you for the length of your sentence," the voice on the vid went on chattily, as if reading my mind. "You need have no concern. Storage facilities beneath the habitat are linked to the central computer system to keep track of consumption. The appropriate packs of food will be delivered throughout the length of your stay. Should you be so foolish as to consume more than your daily ration you will, of course, run out before your sentence is completed. Caution and discipline are suggested."

I thought about this. I believe that the world is divided into two classes of people, hoarders and consumers. There are those who consider a chocolate bar a single unit to be consumed instantly, and there are those who divide it into squares to be portioned out according to some private and personal rule. Gordie, of course, was a consumer, while I was a hoarder. My aim was to make any particular pleasure last as long as possible. I could see trouble down the line, with Gordie bolting his meals and then looking longingly at mine.

The vid demonstrated a boiling water tap and the availability of caffeine-free beverages, and I wondered how Mom in particular would manage to face each morning for eighteen hundred and twenty-six days without her shot of coffee.

There followed a boring description of the environmental controls, the recycling of usable waste, such as paper and plastic dishes, and the disposal of unusable stuff, such as facial tissues. The door at the end of the passage concealed these facilities.

"Paper?" Dad brightened. "I wonder where it's stored and how much of it there is. Enough for a book perhaps?"

My heart sank. If Dad were to decide to write a book while he was here, and if anyone were foolish enough to publish it, I could see us all back in detention when our five years were up. What was it with Dad? I found myself thinking that his singleness of purpose, which I had always admired, was only a way of escaping from reality. Was he actually being selfish?

After all, what about me and Gordie? What were we supposed to do with our time? And Mom too, come to that. She couldn't practise law here, and with nobody but us to argue with I could foresee a tense time ahead. So much for my dream of a happy family. I sighed heavily.

"Should you wish to leave the habitat," the voice went on, "you are, of course, at liberty to do so. It must be emphasized that this is a rehabilitation centre, not a prison. Your World Government is committed to the principles of both freedom and responsibility."

"Huh!" Dad interjected.

"Directions for leaving and returning to the habitat are clearly posted on the exit door. Make sure that you obey these precisely." The vid then ran through them again, in case we were truly stupid, before going on. "Music, appropriate viddisks, games and useful hobby materials are available in the storage units below this screen and around the perimeter of the living area. Exercise disks are also available for your health and enjoyment. You are strongly advised to take advantage of these facilities for both your physical and psychological well-being. We hope that your stay in this correctional unit will be both profitable and pleasant."

The World Government icon filled the screen, accompanied by a stirring rendition of the World Anthem. Then the picture went blank. We sat in silence staring at the empty screen. It had all been so bland, so cosy, so *offensive*. At that moment I felt I would much rather be behind bars in some real prison, watched over by a live prison guard at whom I could get really mad.

Gordie broke the spell. "I'm starving!"

Mom got to her feet. "So let's eat." She went briskly over to the kitchen unit, took out our first breakfast and put the packs into the processor. When it bleeped, she set them on the table. "At least there's no washing-up to fight over. Nothing but forks and spoons. Come and eat, everyone."

Thank goodness Mom is still functioning, I thought. *Maybe it's going to be okay.* But as we sat around the table, Dad began to eat silently, his eyes not moving from the plate in front of him.

"At least we're all together," I ventured.

He grunted. "Not out of the kindness of their hearts, you can bet on that."

"Why not?" Gordie asked. "I was really scared when I woke up alone. Then Alison was there. And you guys." He looked doubtfully from Mom to Dad. "Maybe it's okay. Like a holiday?"

"I was thinking that we'll have a chance to be like a regular family," I stumbled on. "Now that we've got all this time."

Dad snorted. "Time? You sure know how to go for the

21

jugular, Alison. That's my gift to you kids—time! Five years of it!"

Mom's face had flushed. "I don't know what you mean by 'regular family', Alison. It seems to me I've always tried to put you children first, though it hasn't been easy."

"I'm sorry, Mom. I didn't mean . . ." I stopped. Gordie had been right when he'd said things might be tense.

I really wanted to discuss where we were and why, and what we could do with the next five years, but I realized, my heart sinking, that the pattern of silence or bickering wasn't going to be broken overnight.

I sighed, and Gordie must have caught my feeling of frustration. The second he'd finished eating, he slid from his chair. "Can I go outside?"

"Not by yourself."

"Dad, will you take me, *please*?"

"Maybe later." He spoke automatically, and I thought of the countless times he and Mom had put off things we might have done together. It was as if he and Mom had set off together on a train journey, but somehow they had got switched onto different lines moving farther and farther apart. And what about Gordie and me? I figured we were left standing on the station platform.

Was Dad actually afraid to go outside? Afraid of what he might find? He was the reason we were here in this strange prison. If he'd only been more careful . . . Was this what he was thinking? Was he paralyzed with guilt?

"Dad, it'll be okay. It's an adventure, isn't it?" I put a timid hand on his arm, but he shrugged it away.

"Please, Dad. Mom, make him take me outside." Now Gordie was definitely whining, and it was still only the morning of Day One. I guessed it was up to me.

22

"Hey, Gordie, ease up. We've got a whole five years for exploring," I persuaded him. "Don't let's rush into everything the first day. What *I* want to do is find out what games and hobbies that vid was talking about. Let's list them and plan what we're going to do over the next while."

I will say for Gordie that he doesn't have a one-track mind like some little kids I know. Given a reasonable alternative he'll go for it. He snapped out of whine-mode, ran eagerly to the cupboards that lined the curved wall of the living area and began to push aside the sliding doors.

They certainly hadn't stinted, the people who'd furnished our prison. There were blocks of lined paper and boxes of stylos and pencils—*enough writing material for Dad to work on a dozen books*, I thought gloomily. There were art supplies: acrylic paints and pastels and the right kinds of paper for each. There were stencils, construction paper and scissors. Models to build and paint. Fabric, needles and every kind and colour of embroidery yarn. Jigsaw puzzles, both flat and three-D. Hundreds of music disks and maybe fifty viddisks. At one a night, I reckoned we'd only have to rerun these about thirty-five times in the five years we were stuck here. But, of course, we didn't have to watch a vid every night. There were plenty of other family entertainments. Box games, chess and packs of cards.

By the time we had spread all this bounty on the floor, listed it and put it back, we were startled by an electronic voice from the ceiling announcing, "Attention. Twelve noon. Lunchtime, please."

Mom had been looking at some of the fabric I'd

spread on the floor. She jumped. "Good grief! What was that?"

Automatically I looked at my watch. "Monday, July 29, three A.M.," I read aloud. "Boy, is this ever off." I adjusted it. "Twelve noon. But what day?"

Dad did a doubletake. "Mine reads the same. Three in the morning on the twenty-ninth of July."

That was the time the police had called, I remembered. The time we had been zapped. Had they frozen time in some way? What did it mean? *Why*, I thought, suddenly desolate, *we could be anywhere in the world, at any time, and we have no way of knowing.* We were out of the cycle of human living. We were, indeed, among the disappeareds. Like Kristin.

The processor beeped. "Lunch is ready," Mom announced briskly, and we sat down to synthetic meatloaf and anonymous veg. Gordie dug right in, not even complaining about the vegetables.

"I'm going to start on that model space ferry right after lunch," he announced.

"Don't talk with your mouth full, dear," Mom said automatically, but she wasn't angry any more and her mind was obviously on something else. I looked inquiringly at her and she blushed. "Some of those pieces of fabric are gorgeous. An embroidered hanging would really brighten up these walls."

"I didn't know you could do needlework, Mom."

"I was in an arts program before I switched to law, Alison. I had this crazy idea of becoming a famous fabric artist—someone like Beluki, you know."

"So why didn't you?" I put my elbows on the table, my hands under my chin and stared at her. *The things I don't know about my family*, I marvelled. *Mom, the artist. Maybe full of dreams and longings, the way I am.* I realized that I'd never really thought of her as anything except my mom.

She hesitated and I asked again.

She gave a half laugh. "Money, I suppose. Raising a family. I woke up one morning and realized that I'd never be as good as Beluki. So why would anyone want to buy a second-class original when they could get a first-class copy—almost as good as the real thing?"

Parents can be full of surprises, I thought. Then I looked across the table at Dad. *He* hadn't changed. He had grabbed a block of paper and a stylo before I'd tidied everything away again, and was busy making notes, paying no attention to our conversation. I wondered if he even knew that Mom had given up her dream of being an artist so we'd have enough money. *How sad*, I thought. *I would rather she were happy and we were poor.*

As for myself, I wasn't sure what I wanted to do. There were a number of puzzles about the materials we had been given—and I didn't mean jigsaw puzzles, but unanswered questions. How come there were no electronic games? Why no computer—not even an old-fashioned keyboard word processor? I couldn't figure out the answers, but I was dead certain that the choice of games and hobbies wasn't random. In some way these activities were intended to reshape us. Well, that's what a prison sentence was all about, wasn't it? Rehabilitation. An obedient, unquestioning acceptance of World Government and all it stood for. Life in a safe world, peaceful and prosperous, where everyone thought alike.

What I really wanted was a shelf laden with books to browse through. The classics. Novels or biographies. I wasn't fussy. But I hadn't found a single book. When Dad realized this fact, I knew he'd have a fit. Like most writers he was almost as addicted to reading.

"So where's the library?" I challenged him, and he finally looked up and paid attention.

"It's got to be here somewhere," he said at last. "They've thought of everything else."

"I don't believe so. Unless some of the viddisks are books." I checked them through. Lots of classic movies, mostly family-oriented—no crime or police shows, I noticed. And, of course, nothing political.

But no novels.

"Perhaps they're supplied later. A reward for good behaviour. Damn it!" Dad slammed his hand on the table. "A person can't survive without *books*!"

"Maybe there's a library outside," Gordie piped up, and I could see the hope spread across Dad's face like a sunrise. As for me, I didn't believe in any old library "out there". The whole situation was altogether too strange, and I had an uneasy feeling that we were being manipulated, as if we were puppets and someone was pulling the strings to make us dance their way.

Dad got to his feet. "Maybe I *will* take a quick trip outside. Just look around. I won't stay long."

Mom dropped the piece of fabric she had been holding. "Do you think you should? Do be careful, Doug."

"What's to be careful of? Tigers? Probably a lot safer than crossing Main Street back home." He gave a forced laugh.

"Back home you wouldn't have to put on a protective suit and goggles. Think about it, Doug. Suppose this complex has been built in one of the old contaminated zones. It would make sense, wouldn't it?"

"They didn't mention a radiation counter, Carolyn. And there was no warning about it on the door. Or on the vid."

"Can I come too, Dad?"

"Not this trip, son. I'm just going to take a quick look around. I'll take you next time if it's safe."

"Promise?"

"Sure. Cross my heart . . ."

Silently we all watched Dad suit up. The jumpsuit was a perfect fit, and I made a bet with myself that the others would also fit exactly: Mom, who is small and slim, me, tall and big-boned like Dad, and Gordie, a typical skinny eight-year-old. But how did they know ahead of time who would be in this unit?

"You look just like a spaceman, Dad." Gordie watched Dad do up the front zipper. An elasticized hood covered his head tightly, snugging around forehead, cheeks and chin. With goggles and a filter mask over his mouth and nose he looked, I thought, more like a garbage collector than an intrepid explorer. I kept my thoughts to myself though, not wanting to spoil Gordie's romantic notion of Dad heading out into unknown and perilous lands.

"I'm going to close the inside door now. I won't stay long, half an hour max. If it's interesting or if there *are* neighbours out there, I'll report back first before investigating." His voice was muffled by the filter mask.

"Take care. Love you, Doug." Mom's voice shook slightly and I squeezed her hand. It was unexpectedly cold.

"Sure, Carolyn. Me too." I could tell that Dad's mind was already out there, not really taking in what Mom had said. He slid the inner door shut. We were left staring at the blank white wall.

27

"Half an hour's not long, Mom. Time for a cup of coffee?"

"That'd be lovely, Alison."

It wasn't good coffee. It was synthetic and caffeine-free, but Mom didn't seem to notice. She sat at the table, her hands wrapped around the mug, her eyes on the blank white wall that concealed the exit.

Gordie sat on the floor and began to lay out the pieces of the kit he was going to assemble, talking quietly to himself.

I strained my ears to listen past the murmur of his voice, but I could hear nothing from outside but the continual soft scraping sound. What was Dad doing? What was he seeing?

Where are *we*? I asked myself yet again. We had been removed from our apartment in the middle of the night. None of the neighbours had witnessed our arrest. They would have no idea where we had gone. We had become a statistic, four more of the disappeareds, just like those Dad had written about in his Netpaper. Like Kristin and her family.

W*here have we disappeared to*? There were few places left on Earth where a prison camp could be so well concealed that no rumour of its existence would leak out. But obviously there were some. Mom's macabre suggestion that we might be in one of the world's con-taminated zones was a distinct possibility. I shivered and tried to hide my reaction by jumping to my feet.

"More coffee, Mom?"

Mom started and looked down at her mug. "I guess I haven't drunk this yet."

"Don't worry. Dad'll be back soon. Ten minutes to go, that's all."

Just as I finished speaking, Gordie raised his head from his model kit. "What's that funny noise?"

I listened. It seemed to be coming from the wall close to the exit. For a second my heart thumped. Then I remembered. "It's just the vacuum pump, clearing the lock. Dad's back. He's okay!"

Mom leapt up and hurried towards the exit. "He's got to get out of that gear," I reminded her, and she slowed down.

It seemed an age before the inner door slid open and Dad staggered into the room.

"What's happened? Are you all right? You look terrible," Mom cried.

He cleared his throat. "Get me a glass of water, Alison. I'm parched." He dropped to the nearest sofa and we crowded around and watched him drain the glass in one swallow.

"Well?" Mom asked.

He shook his head. "It's a hell-hole out there, Carolyn. Desert. Something like tumbleweed with long thorns. And a wind like you wouldn't believe."

"Any other buildings, Doug? Any neighbours?"

He shook his head again. "Couldn't tell. The sand was so thick I couldn't see a metre in front of me. I walked as far as the tether rope would let me. Getting back with the wind buffeting me was no joke, I can tell you. Nearly swept me off my feet a couple of times. But I didn't see another building, going or coming back."

"We'll just have to wait until the weather clears." Mom put on the bright voice she always used when a case she was defending was going wrong. "Too bad we had to pick a stormy day."

"Right. I'll try again tomorrow."

I wondered why there was no system to tell us what the weather was like *before* we put on all that gear and ventured out. It seemed so stupid. The protective suits and the very existence of the airlock suggested that these sand storms were quite frequent. And why were there no windows in the dome?

I decided to keep my questions to myself, but considered maybe keeping a journal or diary, somewhere I could write them all down. One day it might all come together and make sense. Among the stationery supplies I found a small blank book and defined it as mine by writing my name in it.

ALISON FAIRWEATHER. HABITAT W. ANOTHER PLACE. "SOMEWHERE ON EARTH".

That would have to do for now. Once we had finally gone out and had a chance to explore a bit, I might be able to make a more educated guess at our prison's address.

The speaker came on, startling us once again. "Eighteen hundred hours. It is now suppertime."

I glanced at my watch again. "That's way off. I set my watch at noon and now it's barely five-thirty. Dad . . . ?"

His watch and Mom's both read the same as mine: 17:28.

"So that proves the authorities are manipulating the time for some devious reason of their own," Dad said.

"But why?"

"Who knows." He shrugged.

"Well, I'm hungry," Gordie said definitely, and Mom gave a forced laugh.

"The clock in your stomach seems to keep better time

than our watches. I guess we'll have to trust you, Gordie. And the announcer."

Supper was a repetition of lunch with a differently flavoured sauce over the synthetic meat. Mom had never been a great cook and, especially when she was involved in a big case, Dad and I used to get most of the meals back home. But even our weirder concoctions were more interesting than this. We ate in silence. It was a habit that was hard to break.

After supper we watched a really old movie. As I had suspected, not having any dishes to do made the evening seem even longer. When the movie was over, we just sat. When Gordie said something, I tried to answer, but it wasn't a sparkling family evening. *And it's only Day One.*

The lights suddenly dimmed.

"Uh-oh. Power's out. All that wind," Dad exclaimed.

But it wasn't a power outage. "The lights will go out in thirty minutes," the voice from the ceiling announced firmly. "Those persons intending to shower at night may do so now. Showers are also available on awakening. Remember—one shower only per person per day."

I was beginning to dislike that invisible voice very much—and it was still the first day.

"Bedtime, Gordie. Off you go."

"Do I have to, Mom?"

"Your model will still be here in the morning. No argument, please."

Mom and Dad had their showers. Gordie and I decided we would use the morning times. I had intended to write in my new diary once I was in bed, but the lights went out before I could get around to it. I lay in my prison-issue pyjamas—the same sick green as our overalls—and listened to the whisper that seemed to wrap itself around the dome. I knew now exactly what it was: sand blowing continuously against the plasteel shell of our habitat. Slowly wearing it down. I wondered if the wind out there would ever stop.

CHAPTER THREE

DAY TWENTY-ONE. We have been here for three weeks now. I have no idea of the real date, so I began this diary with DAY ONE. I've been reading through what I've written so far. Not much recently. Very few changes from day to day. For the first week or so Dad went outside every morning right after breakfast and returned, grim-faced, to say that the wind was blowing as hard as ever, and the sand was still obscuring the view so that he could see no farther than a metre or so. "Why don't you try a different time of day?" Mom asked him. "Perhaps the storm is only an early-morning phenomenon." But I know it isn't. I find myself listening to the faint whisper that envelops the dome, sandblasting the plasteel, wearing it away, micron by micron. Sometime in the distant future it will have worn as thin as an eggshell. Maybe it will even collapse, so that whoever is in the prison then will be forced outside. But it won't happen to us. We are only here for five years. Eighteen hundred and twenty-six days minus twenty-one. Eighteen hundred and five. Once Dad had made sure that our isolation was complete—that we were indeed in prison—he seemed to accept our situation, even relish it. He has set up a little writing corner for himself at the end of the bedroom passage, and he writes every day, page after page, as if driven. What's the point? No one will ever publish it.

So Dad writes all day and Mom embroiders. She's

finished one wallhanging that amazes me, a riot of colour that doesn't relate to the mother I remember: the lawyer. Maybe this person is "Carolyn". I stop writing in my diary to ask her this. She smiles, but doesn't answer my question directly. Instead she says, "The curved walls are a problem. I can't hang things from them. Maybe I should do a mural next." While we eat our lunch—a repeat, this diary reminds me, of the lunch we had on our first day and on our eleventh— she stares at the white wall, and I know she is imagining it re-created in paint. As soon as we have finished eating, she begins to make sketches, quick outlines that she scatters over the floor and stares at critically before discarding. I envy her concentration and her ability. But isn't it going in the wrong direction?

What do I expect her and Dad to do, then? Act like parents, I guess. Away from city life, from legal cases and the Netpaper, I had imagined that they might begin to concentrate on Gordie and me. But things haven't changed. They're so absorbed in their own projects that they hardly notice us. If the voice didn't announce mealtimes, they would probably forget to eat. I look at Gordie, who is completing yet another model. The finished fleet of spacecraft is lined up along the top of the storage unit in his room. There's not much space left, but then, there are not that many models left to make. What will he do then? Jigsaw puzzles, perhaps. But all the games in the world aren't enough to fill the days of a lively eight-year-old. Twenty-one days since we arrived here. It must be the middle of August now, I reckon. I've given up looking at my watch. It's gone completely berserk. Back home, school will be starting in a couple of weeks.

Will my friends miss me? Will they even know I'm gone? We only talked about Kristin for a day.

I worried about our education, and a week later I tackled Mom. "What are we going to do about school?"

"Hmm? Why, I don't really know, Alison. There are no books here, are there? Maybe you should ask your father."

I approached Dad warily. He was scribbling away frantically, and I knew he'd snap my head off if I interrupted, so I decided to wait till lunchtime to broach the subject.

"School?" He looked at me blankly, his mind obviously still on his work. "What makes you think that *they* will consider your education of any importance?" His voice was scornful, with a harshness in it I hadn't heard before. Even when he and Mom used to fight over his opinions, his was always the soft, the persuasive voice. I found myself tongue-tied, blushing.

"Well?"

"I don't suppose they do think it's important, since there aren't any textbooks here."

"So you've answered your own question, haven't you, Alison? Now, if you'll excuse me, I have to get back to work."

"No!" I grabbed his arm as he moved to get up. "You've got to listen to me, Dad. It's up to you and Mom to organize schoolwork for Gordie and me. *Five years*! Do you realize that I'll be twenty-one when I get out and Gordie'll be thirteen? We've got to get some sort of education in that time."

"You really think they'll let us go in five years?" His question ridiculed me.

I stared at him and found myself shivering, though the dome was perfectly warm. "Of course. They *have* to. Our sentence will be over. It's against the law if they don't."

"So is arrest, trial and conviction without due process. Wake up, Alison. The so-called justice of World Government is a sham. Have any of the disappeareds ever been released to come back and talk about their time in prison?"

I fought against his words, as if his saying them made them true. "In that case why are you writing this book? What's the point? Why bother if you're never going to get out to see it published and if no one is ever going to read it? At least Mom's mural will brighten up this place a bit, which is a good idea if we're going to be stuck here forever. Though I don't believe that's true, not for a moment."

His lips tightened and I felt the muscle of his arm beneath my hand tighten. His fists clenched. I drew my hand back, suddenly afraid of him for the first time in my life. His eyes blazed and I thought he was going to hit me. Then his eyelids dropped. He shrugged.

"Why do I write? It passes the time." He spoke so softly I barely heard him. Then he left the table to go back to his writing corner. I had noticed that his shoulders had begun to slump and that he was developing a definite pot-belly. There were exercise programs on disks, I remembered, but none of us had taken advantage of them yet. *Maybe we should*, I thought. *Gordie and me anyway*. Meanwhile I realized that asking Dad to educate us was a waste of time.

"Mom, you've got to help us," I begged.

"Yes, dear. Of course. Tell me, Alison, what do *you* think? This design? Or that one?"

They both looked equally crazy to me. "That one." I pointed to the second sketch, not really paying attention. "Mom, Gordie and I need your help."

"Help? Yes, thank you, Alison. You've been a great help. I think I know how to tackle this mural now." She wandered over to the empty white curve of wall. "Yes, I believe I know just what to do."

I wanted to scream. What was *wrong* with Mom and Dad? Back home they sometimes forgot meals and I had to whip up something. But if Gordie and I had stopped going to school, we'd certainly have heard about it. Now it seemed they just didn't care. Almost as if they'd been drugged.

The idea stopped me cold. Mind-altering drugs? Rehabilitation? Once I started thinking about it, the possibility made a lot of sense. But how was the drug administered, and how come it didn't seem to affect me or Gordie? Or did it?

I'm just imagining this, I told myself and made one more attempt to reach out to Mom. I took her by the arm and forced her away from the wall. "You've got to listen to me, Mom. You're putting your work ahead of us. Okay, I do understand, sort of. But you don't have a law practice here. You don't have to put your clients first. You've got us. Your family. Gordie and I, we need your help. Do you understand?" I shook her arm, staring into her face, willing her to pay attention.

For a moment I thought I'd got through. She looked back at me and said slowly, "I'm sorry. I don't think I'm being a very good mother to you, am I?" Then her eyes went cloudy. She smiled vaguely and said, patting my arm, "Being happy, that's what's important, Alison."

She turned back to her mural, and at that moment

Gordie threw the model he'd been working on across the room. "The darn thing won't work. It's stupid. And I'm sick of models, Alison. I'm *bored.*"

Rather than burst into tears, which is what I felt like doing at that moment, I turned on him angrily. "Don't you *dare* whine," I threatened. "All I need right now is a whiny little brother."

"I'm not!" He began to sniffle and for an awful moment I just wanted to hit him. My hands doubled into fists and I turned away, trying to steady my breathing and pull myself together. If I'd been home, I'd have gone for a long walk to cool myself down.

I looked longingly at the outside door. For four weeks we'd been stuck in here and I hadn't even tried to venture outside. That was pretty sick. Where was my ambition? My sense of curiosity? My *courage?*

I made up my mind. "I'm going out, Gordie," I told him. "You're to stay right here and be a good boy until I get back."

"I wanna come too."

"No way. I need some time to myself. Is that clear?" I marched across the room and into the entrance lock, shutting the door behind me. I would have enjoyed the satisfaction of slamming it, but that's something you can't do with a sliding door.

I looked at the suits on their pegs, picked the one that was my size and stepped into it, pulling it up to my waist, shrugging my arms into the sleeves, adjusting the hood and zipping it closed. Anger made me efficient. I snapped on the filter mask and goggles, slid open the outer door and stepped through, closing it carefully behind me.

Freedom, I thought for a split second, and then I was

hit by the overwhelming noise. It wasn't just the wind screaming past, but the incessant small sounds, magnified by the hood tight over my ears, of particles of sand hitting my suit. I took a step away from the dome and the wind swooped down on me, almost throwing me to the ground. I staggered, caught my balance and remembered. *Tether rope.*

I turned back to the whiteness of the dome. The outline of the door was almost invisible, the hand-pull just a faint shadow. There were four ropes coiled against the perimeter wall, half buried in blown sand. I found the loose end of one and attached the ring at its end to the toggle at the waistband of my suit. It closed with a reassuring snap and I turned back again, ready to discover the world "outside".

Dad must be wrong, I told myself. *He didn't venture far enough or widely enough. We're in Habitat W. So where are A to Z? A to V anyway? There must be other domes out here. We can't possibly be alone.*

The sand rose and fell on powerful gusts of wind, sculpted into fragile pillars and veils of brown that moved, changed shape and collapsed as I watched them. Occasionally I had the illusion that there was a clearing, and I would move quickly in that direction, only to be faced with another impenetrable wall of sand, thicker than smog.

This constantly shifting landscape began to make me dizzy and disoriented, and I found myself staggering, out of control. I stopped and stared at the sky above my head. The light was murky, like a three-star pollution day back home, and I had no idea in which part of the sky the sun was actually shining.

I gradually became aware, out of the corner of my

eye, of something shadowy, something that seemed *alive*, but as soon as I turned towards it, it was no longer there. The same thing happened again and again. Each time whatever it was moved too fast for me to identify it. Wild beasts? I wondered. And if so, were they carnivores? If this desert were in North America, they could be coyotes. If we were in Africa, then jackals. But I had heard no wail, no barking laugh. Just the wind howling and the sand pattering against my suit.

Suddenly one of the shadow shapes seemed to turn and come straight for me. I leapt to one side, my heart pounding, but not fast enough. The shape came to rest at my feet and, as I kicked it shudderingly out of my way, I realized that it was nothing more than a tangled sphere of spiky twigs and rootlets. I broke into a hysterical laugh. *The Attack of the Killer Tumbleweeds*, I thought, thankful that there had been no one watching. *The atmosphere of this place is really getting to me. Pull yourself together, Alison.*

I walked on in as straight a line as I could through the arches and pillars of blowing, falling sand, until a sudden tug at my waist brought me to a halt. I had reached the end of the tether and I had seen absolutely no sign of another human habitation.

Instead of retracing my steps as Dad had obviously done, I decided to explore more widely. I turned to my right and began to walk in a slow inward-turning spiral at the limit of the tether. I knew that the rope would wrap itself around the base of the dome and I would eventually find myself back at the entrance. This way I could cover more terrain and if there were another habitat within range, I would be more likely to find it.

The wind had been constantly blowing from the left on

my outward journey. It should now have been blowing from the right. But it wasn't. It blew from behind, pushing me forward. I spread my arms out, feeling like a ship under full sail, and felt it buffet my shoulder blades.

Later, as I circled the dome, reckoning that I was about a quarter of the way around, the wind should have been blowing in my face and then, after that, from the left again. But it wasn't. It blew consistently at my back as if I were walking a straight line instead of a spiral. And the only way that was possible was if the wind itself were blowing in a spiral, round and round, with our dome as its centre. Which, from a meteorological point of view, made no sense at all.

Around I went, with the wind always behind me, until at last I found myself facing the dome, the rope tightly wrapped about its perimeter, and I had to backtrack until I came upon the entrance. My ears were ringing with the pounding of wind and sand. My legs shook, and I had barely enough strength to unclip the tether from my waist, slide open the door of the entrance lock and stagger inside.

Once the outer door was shut behind me, the silence was almost overwhelming. I leaned against the wall, the pounding of my heart shaking my whole body. I reached over and pressed the button marked "vacuum pump". It chugged noisily and I could feel it sucking the sand off my suit. I flipped off goggles and mask, licked my dry lips and blinked my gritty eyes. The thought of water was the only thing that kept me going, that gave me the strength to unzip my suit and peel it off.

The pump turned itself off, and I pushed open the inner door and stepped through, closing it behind me. How good it felt to be home. The faint hiss of sand against the dome was no longer a menace, but a comforting sound that reminded me the storm was *outside*, while we were all safely cocooned *inside*. Warmth. Food. Entertainment.

I staggered over to the kitchen, got myself a long cool drink of water—how good it felt—and looked around. Mother was busy sketching onto the wall the mural she had designed. It was going to be big, some five metres long and over two metres high.

For a moment the triviality of her work made me shake with anger. *Hey, aren't Gordie and I important at all?* I wanted to yell. *I haven't finished growing up myself. I need a little space to be selfish in.* Then I took a deep breath. What I had seen outside was so immense, so appalling, that fussing about who was to look after Gordie seemed suddenly unimportant.

Mom's work was okay if it made her happy, I decided. She had all the time in the world to finish it. Dad was still scribbling in his little corner at the end of the passage. Neither of them had noticed my leaving or my return. Well, that was okay too. I had to learn to let each of them adjust to the situation in their own way.

This left Gordie for me to deal with. He was slouched on the sofa facing the vidscreen. "Oh, there you are, Ally. This is a really dumb movie. I bet I've seen it a zillion times before. I'm bored."

I wasn't mad any more. I realized that my education was going to be frozen at age sixteen, but there was no reason for Gordie to face the same fate. I would be his teacher.

"You're not going to be bored any more," I told him firmly. "You're going back to school."

"I am? Who's going to teach me?" He looked doubtful.

I saw a small window for argument, but closed it right away. "I am. Everyday from now on. You're not going to have time to be bored."

"Oh. Will I like it?"

"Of course you will. We'll have fun, I promise you." I hoped I sounded more positive than I felt as I tried to remember what I had learned so long ago, back in Grade Four.

Luckily the voice chose that moment to announce, "Eighteen hundred hours. It is now suppertime."

I went to the kitchen and pulled out the next four meals. 28. 3. M. F. FC. MC. Supper on the twenty-eighth day of our incarceration. Meal for Dad, Mom, myself and Gordie. As I slipped them into the processor, I suddenly had the weird thought that it would be very easy to drug us through our food. Everyday, three times a day, we each ate the food intended specifically for us. Was this what was happening? Was this why Mom and Dad were becoming more and more distant from us, more uninterested in us, while Gordie and I were still okay?

The more I thought about it, the more certain I was that I was right. But what could I do about it? Warning Mom and Dad would be useless. They didn't even listen to the normal things I said to them. I could just imagine their reaction to the idea that they were being manipulated through drugs in their food. And what could they do about it anyway? They couldn't stop eating, and there was no source of nourishment other than the food already prepared for us. I thought of trading my meal with Mom's. But suppose it turned me into a zombie and I didn't even remember that I'd switched the meals? That was a scary thought.

The processor pinged, and I put all four trays on the table and went to call Dad, who hadn't even heard the announcement. "Go ahead and start eating," I urged him. "I need to get something from my room."

As soon as he'd turned the corner, I ducked back and looked at what he'd been writing for the past month. He already had a fair-sized stack of paper. The early part, in his normal tight scholarly hand, was what I would have expected from the investigative reporter who had got us into this mess in the first place. But recently the writing had begun to change. The script was larger, with more generous loops and capitals. The subject matter also seemed to have shifted. It was no longer an argument in favour of a more democratic society, but a crazy Utopian fantasy. It didn't even make sense.

That's it, I thought. *He's been drugged into la-la land, and there's nothing I can do about it.*

It was a grim idea, and it made me mad. *I'm only sixteen,* I protested inwardly. *I'm too young to be both Mom and Dad in this family.*

I was partway through my supper when I thought: *Maybe Gordie and I are being drugged too.* I gagged on a mouthful of synthetic protein and had to jump up and get a glass of water.

"Are you okay, Ally?" Gordie asked. "Did you choke on a crumb?"

I swallowed. "No, I'm fine." *But what about you, Gordie?* I thought. *Are they doing anything to you?* I couldn't detect anything wrong—he seemed to be the same old Gordie I loved and who drove me crazy—but how did I *know*?

Gordie's schooling went pretty smoothly for a while. I

worked with him every morning, dredging up memories of English and math, reciting to him all the bits of my favourite poems that I could remember, and then setting him some exercises to do in the afternoon. This gave me an hour to rest. I'd been feeling really tired recently, plagued by frightening nightmares of dust storms and tumbleweeds that must have been seeded in my subconscious during that expedition outside.

After I had checked his work every afternoon, we exercised for an hour with one of the viddisks, and then we played board games together. At first we found these rather boring because they were so unlike the competitive games we were used to—ACQUISITIONS and MARKET FUTURES, tense ones like those. These games were set in fantasy situations where the players earned more points by cooperating with each other than by going it alone. This was a hard lesson for us to learn, but as we grew more skilled, the idea began to grow on us. The game Gordie particularly liked was set in a sort of paradise with fruit trees for the picking and fish to be netted from pollution-free streams.

"It's like Xanadu," Gordie said suddenly during a game.

Xanadu. The ancient poem had been one of my favourites in high school. We had not studied it in English class because the teacher said it was too incoherent, that the poet—Coleridge, his name was—had been pretty well spaced-out when he wrote it. But our art teacher played the audio-disk during class and asked us to free-paint whatever the words made us think of. I loved it, and it was one of the poems I often recited to Gordie during English lessons until he knew all the words too.

Thinking of school made me miss my friends and the life that I knew in my heart I would never regain; but mostly I found myself remembering Kristin. Her sassiness. Her obstinacy. Her way of cutting through pretence. *You're so naive, Alison.*

"Your turn to play, Ally," Gordie reminded me.

In Xanadu did Kubla Khan a stately pleasure-dome decree . . . Xanadu. It had always been my private and personal fantasy—to someday find that magic place where "walls and towers were girdled round", so far removed from the high-rise plasteel buildings and the canyon streets of my hometown. "What made you think of Xanadu?"

Gordie shrugged. "Dunno."

We went on playing.

"It's like a dream place," he said after a while. "It's out there, you know." He pointed to the exit door. No one had opened it since my exploration. I had promised myself that if a moment came when I no longer heard the continual scuff of sand against the dome, I would venture outside again. But that moment had not yet come. The wind never ceased to blow. The sand scrubbed the white skin of the dome, and I was sure that the tumbleweeds still whirled past in their ghostly spiral dance.

I shivered. "There's nothing out there but sand, Gordie. I *told* you. You know that."

He shook his head obstinately and moved his piece forward on the board. "One day I'm to go out and find it." His voice was so certain that it really scared me. Was this *his* delusion?

"Not without me you won't," I snapped. "I mean that, Gordie."

He smiled at me, a knowing kind of smile. "If the

dream tells me to, then I'll have to go, Ally, won't I?"

I pushed the board aside, completely rattled. "*Have* to go? You don't *have* to go anywhere. You've got to stay in the dome, where it's safe . . ." Then I did a doubletake. "Dream? What dream? What are you talking about, Gordie?"

He patted my hand in this new, suddenly confident manner, as if our roles were reversed, as if he were the older and wiser. "It's all right, Ally, really. Don't *you* have the dream too? I know Mom and Dad can't, but I thought perhaps you would."

I shook my head. "I don't dream. Not like that. Just little snippets of memory." I wasn't going to tell him my nightmare—the one in which I am out in the dust storm and the tumbleweeds come alive . . .

"If the dream tells you to go outside, will you promise to call me first, Gordie?"

He thought about it seriously and then shook his head. "I don't think I can, Ally. Not unless you have the dream too."

I stared at him. He wasn't being cheeky or putting me on. His blue eyes looked straight into mine, and I knew he was telling me the simple truth—that if the dream called him, he'd have to go. And there would be no way of stopping him. Our strange prison had no locks on any of the doors.

I looked at him in a kind of panic. I could watch him every minute of the day and make sure he didn't try to escape. But at night? I couldn't exist without sleep. If only I could make Mom and Dad see the danger, we could take it in turns to guard him. But that was hopeless. I knew I was on my own.

The only antidote to Xanadu that I could think of was

a dose of the real world out there. I made up my mind quickly. "Come on, Gordie. We're going outside."

"Really? Now?" The grave grown-up expression dropped away and his face shone with simple small-boy enthusiasm.

"Yes, right now." I grabbed his hand and pulled him into the entrance lock, sliding the door shut behind us. I lifted down the smallest suit from its hook and showed him how to climb into it, how to adjust the hood and then close the zip-front. "And don't forget your face mask and goggles, no matter how excited you are."

He nodded, jogging from one foot to the other while I climbed into my dust-proof jumpsuit and put on my own mask and goggles.

"Out we go." I pulled open the outer door and felt the force of the wind battering at me. I clipped on our tether ropes quickly before Gordie could blow away. "And remember to close the door behind you, Gordie. That's important. Or the lock might fill with sand and you'd have trouble getting back in."

"But I won't be coming back, Ally." His voice blew away on the wind.

I pulled him close and shouted in his ear. "Oh, Gordie, be realistic! Look at it. *This* isn't Xanadu." I waved a hand at the desolation around us.

Nothing had changed from before. The pillars and falling veils of dust enveloped us. The ghostly shapes scudded silently by. I remembered my nightmare and pushed the memory aside, concentrating on Gordie.

"Let's take a little walk before we go back." I took his hand, leading him forward in the direction I had taken the time before.

He pulled his hand out of mine. "Not that way, Ally."

He turned confidently to the left and began to run into the storm. In only a second he had vanished. I panicked and screamed, "Gordie, come back!" before remembering his tether. I grabbed hold of it and followed him, running until he appeared again through the clouds of sand.

He saw me and tried to run again, but was knocked to the ground by a particularly powerful gust of wind. I helped him to his feet. I could see, behind his goggles, the tears running down his cheeks.

"It's out there, Ally. I know it is. Not far away."

"Then we'll find it together, Gordie. Come on." I took his hand firmly in mine, and we went forward together, Gordie tugging insistently until we came, as I knew we must, to the end of our tether ropes.

"That's as far as we can go," I shouted as cheerfully as I could.

He peered into the gloom. "It's out there somewhere, Ally. Just a little way away."

"We can't see it today. I expect we have to wait for a day when the wind finally drops. If that happens we'll be able to see Xanadu. Right now, we've got to go back to the dome."

As we retraced our steps, Gordie walked slowly, scuffing his feet in the sand, stopping now and then to look over his shoulder. His belief in Xanadu was so strong he almost had me convinced. If I hadn't kept a firm grip on his hand, he'd have run back.

When we reached the entrance, I slid open the outer door and pushed Gordie in before undoing his tether. I didn't trust him not to make a bolt for it. I shut the door and turned on the vacuum pump.

"Okay. Goggles and mask off. And now the suit."

He said nothing, but stood there like a dummy and let me strip off his jumpsuit. I slid open the inner door. Nothing had changed. Mom was painting her wall. Dad was in his corner, writing.

"Xanadu is only a dream, Gordie," I said firmly. Then, as I looked around the familiar dome, I thought it seemed as unreal as Xanadu. Seventeen hundred and seventy days to go, I reminded myself. "Only a dream," I repeated, and I wanted to weep, so strong was my sense of loss.

"Yes, Ally." I could see the corners of his mouth droop. The stains of dried tears were on his cheeks.

I put my arms around him. "I'm so sorry," I whispered. "I wish Xanadu were real, truly I do."

The nightmare came back that night, brought on, I suppose, by our search for Xanadu. This time it began with me standing outside, knowing I was some distance from the dome, although I couldn't see it. I was surrounded by tumbleweeds. Their dark spheres broke open to show red mouths edged with jagged teeth. Their thorns elongated into fierce claws. In my dream I turned to run back to the dome, to safety. But my tether rope was gone and I had no idea which way safety lay. I ran anyway, my feet sticking like glue, moving more and more slowly. When I looked down, I could see that my feet and ankles were buried in sand. As I watched, I sank farther. Now the sand was almost up to my knees, and I knew I was going to be buried alive in it.

I yelled and sat up in bed, shaking and sweating. What a dream! Had I woken anyone, or was the yell only part of the nightmare? I listened and could hear nothing. Nothing but the air conditioning and the gritty whisper of the sand outside.

I got out of bed and went to the kitchen for a drink. Though the dome was always in darkness at night, there was a nightlight in the passage that gave a comforting glow, enough for me to see my way. I drank the water slowly, telling myself firmly that, indeed, it had only been a dream. It was over and it would not come back.

I still felt edgy and my thoughts turned to Gordie. I tiptoed down the passage and quietly opened his door. It was all right. I could see the hump of his sleeping body under the bedclothes. I padded back to my own room and eventually went to sleep.

When the wake-up call came, I was feeling completely frazzled, as if I hadn't slept at all. I was glad that Gordie had the first shower. I lay with my eyes shut, half listening for the pad of his feet down the passage, for the sound of the shower.

Bother. He must have overslept too, I thought, and struggled reluctantly out of bed and down the passage. "Wake up, sleepyhead."

He didn't stir, so I went in and shook his shoulder. "Come on, Gordie, time to get going."

The shape under the bedclothes disintegrated in my hands into a pillow and a rolled-up blanket. Just for a moment I didn't allow myself to believe what I knew had happened. *Great joke, Gordie. But not today. Not when I feel so rotten.*

"Come out, wherever you are," I called, my voice shaking. I listened to the silence and my pounding heart. Then I raced down the passage to the exit and pulled the inner door open. *Don't let it have happened,* I prayed.

But it had. The small suit was gone. The goggles and the mask, both gone. I ran back, shouting, "Mom! Dad! Gordie's gone outside!"

They blinked at me, not understanding.

"Outside!" I yelled again. "Alone!"

For a second I thought I'd cut through the drug barrier to the people underneath. I thought I saw understanding in their dazed eyes. A flash of panic.

"Eight a.m. Time for breakfast," the disembodied voice interrupted, and it was as if a veil slipped down over their faces.

"Time for breakfast, Alison," Mom said. "Why, you're not even dressed yet."

"Mom, Gordie's *gone*."

"Then he'll miss breakfast, won't he? They won't be pleased."

"He'll *die* out there. Dad, you remember what it's like!"

He hesitated, then shook his head. "There's nothing we can do, Alison."

I turned away, full of terrible anger as well as despair. I wanted to shake them, make them understand. I clenched my hands so tightly that the nails bit into my palms. Their behaviour was proof of the drugs, all right. I took a deep breath. It was up to me, wasn't it?

I scrambled into my clothes and made for the exit. As I climbed into my protective gear I still shook with anger and had to keep telling myself, *They can't help it. It's the drug, not them.*

I slid the outer door shut behind me and leaned back against it, afraid to move. Outside was like my nightmare all over again. Only now it was real . . .

CHAPTER FOUR

Was the wind really blowing more violently than before? Was the sand driving at me more viciously, or was it just my imagination? I strained my eyes for a glimpse of Gordie, trying to penetrate the whirling bands and columns of sand. I shouted, and my voice, muffled by my filter, was picked up by the wind and tossed away.

How long had he been gone? All night? What chance did he have in this storm? I remembered how he had been blown to the ground the day before, when I had been there to help him. How was I to help him now? How could I even find him?

Then I remembered the tethers. If Gordie had listened to my lesson yesterday afternoon, he would have fastened a tether to his suit. Sure enough, one of the four ropes lay uncoiled, pointing as straight as a ruled line over to the left, in the direction where Gordie had said Xanadu was to be found.

I fastened a tether to the toggle on my own waistband and began to run, head down, my body buffeted by the wind as I tried to force my way through it. A tumbleweed rolled by, and when one skidded against my leg, I was back in the horror of my nightmare.

Forget that, I told myself firmly. *It was only a dream.* I gritted my teeth and ran on, my eyes on Gordie's tether, as the wind tried constantly to blow me off course, to send me round to the right. *Gordie is the only thing that matters. Follow the rope and he'll be there, at its end.*

Although I tried to keep this picture clearly in my mind, dark questions, like the shadowy tumbleweeds, kept creeping into my head. Why was Gordie's tether rope lying slack on the ground? If he were out there, moving around, surely I would notice some movement, even a quiver. But the rope never budged.

I was suddenly jerked to a standstill and fell to my knees. I had come to the end of my own tether rope. I scrambled to my feet. "Gordie!" I yelled again, and my heart leapt with relief when a shadowy figure appeared in front of me. I held out my arms to embrace it, but it dodged to one side and whirled on. Only another pillar of sand, mocking me.

I looked down and saw, almost at my feet, what I dreaded most of all. It was the end of Gordie's tether, the metal ring gleaming faintly in the dim light. I picked it up and stared at it, willing it to be a mistake. *Only a dream. This is all only a dream,* I told myself. But I could feel the weight of rope in my hand, the coldness of the metal ring even through my gloved fingers. It was all too real. And so was the fact that Gordie had slipped off the restraint and vanished into the storm.

"It's out there somewhere," he had said. "Just a little ways off."

Xanadu? Or death?

My eyes were filling with tears and I automatically raised my hand to scrub them away. But my hand encountered only the goggles. The tears were running down inside, a sticky layer between my cheekbones and the plastic frame.

"If the dream tells me to, then I have to go, Ally."

And I have to follow, I told myself grimly. Quickly, not giving myself time to think about what I was doing, I unclipped the tether from my waist and laid the rope end carefully on the ground next to Gordie's, two parallel lines leading back to the dome. It would be a clear signal to Mom and Dad when they came looking for us.

But they're not going to come. You know that, Alison. You're on your own.

All right. A signal to us then, to Gordie and me, when I've found him. The way back to safety.

With a mental picture of Gordie alive and well, only a few metres away from me, I stumbled forward, trying to keep in a straight line away from the dome, despite the efforts of the wind to blow me off course into its spiralling clockwise path.

I was afraid, desperately, mouth-dryingly afraid. But at the same time my body felt a kind of excitement. Now there was no restraint at my waist, pulling me back to the dome, reminding me that I was a prisoner. I was free for the first time since that night in July when the knock at our apartment door had changed our lives forever.

Freedom. I tried to keep this idea in the front of my mind. *Freedom and Xanadu.* I muttered the magic words to myself, trying to push the fear away:

"And there were gardens bright with sinuous rills,
Where blossomed many an incense-bearing tree;
And here were forests ancient as the hills,
Enfolding sunny spots of greenery . . ."

My imagination was so strongly stirred I could smell the incense trees and, through the turmoil of wind and sand, I thought I could hear the murmur of little streams.

My skin suddenly prickled all over and I smelled, not incense, but ozone. My brain instantly reacted, throwing my body backwards. WARNING, it said. Electrical interference!

No, I told myself. *I have to go on. I have to find Gordie. But—ahead lies unknown danger.*

As I hesitated, I became aware of a new sensation. Silence. The wind had died. The sand no longer beat against my suit and obscured my vision. Surely I should be able to see Gordie if he were nearby . . .

I tore off my goggles, blinked and rubbed my teary eyes. Then I blinked again, this time in disbelief. Directly in front of me was a silvery shimmering curve. I turned around. Behind me the storm raged on, the air filled with veils and columns of sand.

I turned again, trying to make sense of what I had glimpsed. It was like being inside a vast soap bubble, enclosing the savage microclimate of sand storms that circulated the dome at its heart, the dome that was our prison.

When I had freed myself from my tether, I had broken out of that first dome like an unfledged bird out of its egg. Could I break through this gossamer bubble, this second shell, and become truly free? Like Gordie, if Gordie were out there?

"I won't be coming back," he had told me with such chilling certainty.

Then I must come to you, Gordie, I told myself, and strode forward with my hands out in front of me.

What had I expected? A pop, like the bursting of a party balloon and the collapse of an illusion? I'm not sure.

What actually happened was a brilliant spark. A hiss. A stinging pain in my fingertips and a numbness right up my arms. The bubble was still intact. I hadn't even grazed it.

I drew back, rubbing my arms. The fingertips of my gloves were crinkled as if I'd touched an overhot iron. I moved a metre or so along the perimeter and cautiously prodded at the bubbly film again. This time the stinging in my fingers was worse and my arms ached the way they do when you hit your funny bone. Not a life-threatening pain, but for a few minutes excruciating.

It was hopeless. Gordie was free and I was still in prison. But I couldn't let that happen. He was a bright boy, but he was only eight years old and he *needed* me. Even in a dream kingdom. Even in Xanadu he needed me.

And, I realized, I needed him too. I could not bear to return to the dome without him, to face the unchanging daily routine of announced meals and set bedtimes, with a father and mother who were no longer the Mom and Dad I had grown up with, loved, hated and argued with, but who were now more like a couple of drugged strangers.

"Gordie got through," I said aloud. "So I must be able to."

I remembered his shining face, his eager eyes, as he spoke of Xanadu. What would he have done when he first came upon the silvery bubble?

I could almost hear him say, "Go for it, Ally!" I took a deep breath and ran forward as fast as I could.

Xanadu, I thought as I ran. *Xanadu*.

There was a brilliant flash. A pain like molten metal ran right through my bones. I screamed. And then, mercifully, I blacked out.

SOUND. I'd read somewhere that sound is the last of the senses to vanish when one is dying. And the first to

come to an unborn baby. Was I dying? Or being reborn?
I could hear the rustle of leaves. Water running between
pebbles, a sound that was almost a chuckle. The call of
a bird, unfamiliar, but then there were few birds in the
city nowadays, and the ones in the aviary at the zoo
were a sad lot, not much inclined to celebration. This
was true music, a trilling melody repeated with variation after variation; a composition in progress.

SMELL. Wet stones. Fresh grass. The mixed perfume
of many kinds of flowers. Behind all these hung a haunting exotic scent. *Incense-bearing trees.* I was in Xanadu!
I had made it.

I opened my eyes to a new green world and sat up,
only to find the green spinning round and round. I
groaned and fell back, shutting my eyes and swallowing
sudden nausea.

"Lie still. Moving will only make you feel worse."

At the sound of the strange voice I opened my eyes
again, but all I could see was the dark silhouette of a
man kneeling beside me. He laid a cloth over my forehead. Cold and wet. I licked my dry lips. "Thirsty," I
whispered, and wonderful water was squeezed into my
mouth, drop by drop.

I must have drifted into a state that was part uncon-
sciousness, part dream, for when I surfaced again the
man was talking. He had a light voice, matter-of-fact
and reassuring.

". . . force field not tuned to your mass, far too powerful for you. Lucky you weren't badly hurt. Now that
you've had a few hours rest, you should be ready to
travel soon."

"Force field?" I hung on to the one word that seemed
important.

"Surrounding your habitat. You broke right through it. Brave but foolish, Alison."

I opened my eyes and struggled up on one elbow. My head still swam, but not as violently as before. Was I hallucinating? I seemed to be lying on the flowery bank of a stream, broad trees above giving a welcome shade to my sensitive eyes. Beside me a man sat cross-legged on the mossy turf. He wore a motley collection of fabrics that fluttered in the breeze and gave an over-all impression of iridescent blue-black, though the pieces were many-coloured. His blond hair lay smoothly against his head except right on top, where it stood up in a quiff that gave him the appearance of a small boy.

Like Gordie. Where is *Gordie?* The thought floated through my spinning head and then vanished again. I stared, blinking. The stranger was quite grown-up in fact, though his actual age was a puzzle. In some lights his face appeared smooth, but when the sun caught it at an angle I could see wrinkles around the eyes and lines at the corners of his mouth. I had never seen him before in my life.

"How do you know I'm Alison?"

"That's my business."

I flushed. "I was only asking."

"I meant that it is my business to know. Your name— everything about you."

"Oh. So, what's *your* name?"

He shrugged as if his name were of no importance and smiled. It was a very endearing smile, but I wasn't sure I entirely trusted it. "You can call me Jay."

My head was finally beginning to clear and I could think straight again. "If you know all about me, you must know about my brother, Gordie. He's only eight years old. Just a little kid. Is he here in Xanadu? Is he safe?"

"Perfectly safe. He came through without any problem. We were expecting him."

Expecting him. What did he mean? I struggled to my knees. "Where is he? I want to see him."

"As soon as you're strong enough to walk, I'll take you to the village."

"I'm fine now," I said obstinately and got to my feet, swaying. "Really I am."

He laughed gently. "Very well. Put your arm through mine. There. Now we go this way . . ."

I had a kaleidoscopic impression of exotic trees silhouetted against an intensely blue sky. Of grass, short, dense, springy beneath my feet, of a path winding downwards into a valley. At times we approached a stream that chattered eagerly beside us. Once we crossed it on smooth stepping stones, Jay holding my hand to steady my still-wobbly legs to the other side.

Then the trees grew farther apart, and in the distance, just below us, I could see a glade, the haze of a fire. There was the smell of smoke. Another mouthwatering smell, strong and heady, of roasting meat. And above it all the shrill sound of eager children's voices, many voices. I pulled my arm away from Jay's and began to stumble downhill.

"Gordie!" I called. "Gordie, are you there? It's Ally."

A group of about thirty children turned their faces towards us. Most of them seemed to be between the ages of eight and ten, though a couple looked younger, and two or three were definitely older. They wore the same kind of overalls as mine, but in a motley collection of colours, variously light and dark blue, bottle green, orange, red and purple.

"It's Jay! He's brought another one. Two in one day!"

As they ran eagerly towards us, I looked for Gordie among them. No light green overalls. No quiff of dark hair. The other children stared at me—coldly it seemed—but clustered around Jay, tugging at his sleeves, pulling on his tunic, chattering all the time in their shrill voices.

"She's not one of us, Jay!"

"She's a grown-up, like the other."

I whirled around to face Jay. "Where *is* he? You told me he was safe!"

Jay raised a hand and there was instant obedient silence. "Where is Gordie?" he asked, and a chorus of eager voices answered him.

"He's new, so we gave him the most important job."

"He's turning the spit."

"And we told him not to stop . . ."

"Or the beast might burn."

Jay laughed. "Well done. Let's show our friend Alison where he is."

It seemed to me that the looks the children gave me were wary, even unfriendly, as if I were someone to be afraid of. "Grown-up", they'd said. And "like the other one". But they obediently led the way downhill towards the glade, with many of them still holding on to a piece of Jay's clothing.

I held out a hand to one youngster on the edge of the crowd, but she shied away and ran on, giggling, with the others. For a second I felt rejected, but then it didn't matter, for I could see the stone fireplace at the centre of the clearing, and the small green-clad figure turning the spit. Everything else was forgotten in the rush of thankfulness that he was safe.

"Gordie!" I ran across the grass, holding out my arms, wanting to hug him, to hold him tight and prove to myself that he was real and not a dream—that Xanadu wasn't a dream. He wouldn't let go of the big handle that turned the spit, not even for a hug, but his face was one big smile, and that made up for everything.

"Hullo, Ally. I'm glad you could come. I wasn't sure . . . The others said that old people couldn't come into Xanadu. I thought I'd never see you again, and I cried. So they gave me the job of seeing that the roast doesn't burn. It's most important. This is real meat, you know, not synprotein. Jay hunted it with his bow and arrow and brought it to us. Doesn't it smell wonderful? Aren't you hungry?"

I was laughing, but at the same time my eyes were swimming with tears. I wiped them away with the back of my hand. "That darn smoke," I explained. "Yes, I'm starving. And the others were wrong. I got through, so I guess that proves I'm not too old."

"You won't try to make me go back, will you, Ally? 'Cause I'm not going, so there!" There was an edge to his voice that startled me.

"Of course I won't. Only . . ." My voice faded as I thought of Mom and Dad in that dreary dome, caught up in their compulsions: Dad writing and rewriting reams of stuff that would never get published; Mom painting meaningless murals that would be seen by no one except Dad, who didn't take his nose out of his notes long enough to notice them.

"Only what about Mom and Dad?" I went on. "We can't leave them alone back there, in prison, can we?"

"I . . . I don't know, Ally. There aren't any grown-ups here. Just us. And Jay, of course. He'll know. I'll ask Jay if he can bring them to Xanadu as well. I'll ask him right now! You turn the handle." He darted through the crowd of children and shook Jay's arm. "Ally's here. You brought her after all! So can you please bring our mom and dad out too?"

His voice was no louder than any of the others, but an abrupt silence followed his question. All eyes turned first to him and then to Jay. A sudden hiss of fat and a flare of flame pulled me back to my duty, and I grabbed the handle and began to turn the meat on the spit, all the time watching and listening.

What was wrong with Gordie's simple request? For something certainly was. The eyes of all the children were on me now. Hostile eyes. I knew uneasily that I was not one of them. To them I was an adult. I was on the other side. "Enemy" seemed too strong a word, but that was the message their eyes sent me. *You're the enemy.*

I swallowed my own anger and concentrated on turning the spit while I waited for Jay's answer.

"You haven't been with us long enough to know the rules of this place, Gordie." Jay spoke gently. "The children will tell you."

"This is *our* place."

"We're in charge, not the grown-ups."

"*We* make the rules."

"We all have to agree before we change anything."

"We co . . . co . . ."

"Cooperate." Jay smiled. "So you see, Gordie, you can't ask me to do anything as serious as allowing grown-ups to be part of this place. You have to ask the other children."

"After supper," someone suggested. "We should hold a council after supper."

There was a chorus of agreement and I began to think that perhaps a society governed by children might work. But what about *my* place here? I had a feeling that I wouldn't be part of any council, that my advice wouldn't be sought. And I seemed to be the only teenager. *Suppose they won't let me stay?*

My thoughts were interrupted by four youngsters crowding around me. "It's okay. You can stop turning the spit."

"It's cooked now and we're going to eat."

Politely, but definitely, they elbowed me out of the way. Two of them held a huge wooden platter ready to catch the roast as the other two struggled to lift it off the spit. I wanted to help, but something told me that would not be a good idea. With difficulty, but with no accidents, they staggered with their load to a long wooden table that ran down the centre of the glade, some distance from the fireplace.

Meantime other children were busy hauling big steaming pots from the edge of the fire. The very smallest kids each carried three or four wooden plates and laid them along the sides of the table. I counted. There seemed to be about thirty places in all.

Jay, still surrounded by a bevy of children, approached the table, and the rest of the children scrambled onto benches on either side. My mouth watered and my stomach clenched in hunger, but I stood back, unsure of my welcome.

"This is Alison." Jay introduced me.

"My big sister, Ally," Gordie added proudly.

"Where shall she sit?"

There was whispered discussion, and then room was made for me between Gordie and a small girl whose name, I later found out, was Meredith—Merry for short.

Jay picked up a carving knife and fork. "And who will carve today?"

A girl of about nine stood up. "It's my turn today, Jay."

"Do you remember the safety rules, Anna?"

She nodded eagerly. "Always cut away from you. Always hold the roast steady with the fork. And make sure the sticky-out bit on the fork is out."

"The guard. That's perfect, Anna."

The small girl climbed on a stool and began to carve the roast. I watched and worried, knowing that Mom and Dad would never have allowed Gordie to touch a carving knife—if indeed we'd had anything to carve. Meanwhile various side dishes of vegetables I could not identify were passed along the table. I watched Meredith to see how much she took and made sure to help myself to no more.

"The food is great," Gordie whispered as I passed the platters on to him. "You should have been here for lunch!"

"Where does it come from? Where are the stores?" I whispered back, but he shrugged. "It's Xanadu" was all he said.

I looked for knife and fork, saw neither and copied my neighbours, picking up the food in my fingers. Soon I was too busy eating to ask questions, or even to think about our strange situation.

How can I describe roast meat? The outside was crackly and brown, and beneath was a layer of creamy fat that melted softly, while the meat itself filled my mouth with juice. When I had eaten a single slice of it, I felt more satisfied than with any food I had ever eaten before.

I suddenly remembered a time when I was even younger than Gordie and Great-Grandfather was reminiscing about something he called a bar-bee-cue. They used to have it on special feasts when he was a very small boy, he had said, in the days when there were still farmers, before the World Government instituted chemically produced foods for everyone. I wondered if this wonderful meat tasted anything like that.

When the roast meat was finished and the vegetables eaten, a bowl of real fruit was passed along the table. It was strange to eat, this fruit from Xanadu. It had a skin that was firm—kind of like edible plastic—with soft, incredibly juicy flesh inside. In the centre was a hard oval. "Why would they make fruit like this, with a lump of wood in the middle?" I asked Merry.

She laughed. "It's called a pit. If you plant it, a tree will grow with the same kind of fruit on it."

I wondered if she knew what she was talking about. It seemed incredible. I stared at the grooved object, the "pit", and imagined it containing the secret for remaking itself. Then I remembered a long-ago botany lesson and realized that this must be a "seed".

"Don't worry about it, Ally. It's Xanadu," Gordie said confidently, as if that were the answer for everything—and for him, I suppose it was.

When the meal was over, all the children tidily took their plates, emptied bones and pits into the fire and stacked the dishes. The leftover slices of meat were hung above the fire to dry, only a platter of vegetables and scraps of meat remaining at the end of the table. *If they don't put that in a fridge, it'll spoil,* I thought. But I kept quiet. It was none of my business.

"Whose turn is it to wash up?" someone asked.

"Mine."

"And mine to dry. But perhaps we should hold the council first, before it gets dark?"

In the moment's silence that followed this suggestion, I spoke up. "Would it help if I did the dishes?"

They looked at each other. There was a chorus of assent and I found myself with a pile of greasy dishes and some pots. Water had been heated while we ate, and one of the kids emptied a handful of jellylike stuff into the hot water. It foamed up, like syndet, and with a thick felty leaf from some kind of bush or tree I was able to scrub the dishes clean. It was interesting, different from stacking plates in the dishwasher or recycling them, as we did in the dome.

Where did the pots come from? I wondered as I scrubbed. They were made of iron. They hardly fit into the "back to nature" philosophy of this camp, with wooden plates and no knives and forks. Maybe there was a city not far away, and when the camp-out was over, the campers would all go home. Even though this made a kind of sense, somehow I doubted it.

The children had disappeared among the trees at the edge of the glade to hold their council, and I was alone and amazingly happy. No prison. No sand gritting eternally against the outside of the dome. Freedom. That was it! The combination of splendid food, clean mild air, the rustle of trees and chatter of birds to keep me company conspired to make me feel I was indeed in Xanadu. And, above all, Gordie was safe.

I was still stooping over the pots when a movement

behind me made me turn. Close to the table stood a girl of about my own age. She ignored me, hastily gobbling up the shreds of meat and the broken bits of vegetables that had been left, stuffing them into her mouth with both hands.

She was taller than I was, with an unruly tangle of greasy blonde hair and a dirt-smudged face. Unlikely though it was, she looked vaguely familiar. When she saw me staring, her face turned suddenly scarlet. She straightened up, wiping her soiled hands on the front of her overalls, already stained and stiff with grease, and came closer.

"Alison? Alison Fairweather? It *is* you, isn't it?"

I blinked. "*Kristin*? Is it really you? What happened to you? How did you get here?"

She shrugged. "The same way you did, of course. Courtesy of the World Government Police. So the famous Fairweathers were not immune after all." She gave a sarcastic laugh.

I flushed at her tone of voice. "What's that supposed to mean?"

She smiled coldly. "People used to say that the award-winning journalist and the human-rights lawyer with the genuine gold halo were untouchable. But I see WOGPO got you in the end."

In one way Kristin hadn't changed a bit, I realized. Just as direct and sarcastic as ever. I tried to ignore her attitude. She had always been a know-it-all. Maybe she had the answers to some of my questions. "Kristin, when you disappeared, I went to your apartment to ask for you. There was another family there. They said I must have mistaken the address—as if I could! But you weren't in the phone directory any more. It was so weird. After a while I began to wonder if I'd imagined you."

"And now here you are, in the same boat. That's a joke." Her laugh was definitely unfriendly. Why? We'd been best friends before, hadn't we? I bit back a cross answer and found myself wondering who might be left to worry about Dad and Mom, Gordie and me. My grandparents, of course. Would the police have left Gran and Gramps in peace or would they be watching them, harrying them? Would my school friends miss me or was I already forgotten in the excitement of a new school year? And what about Dad's fellow writers and those readers who followed his work on the Net? And Mom's colleagues down at Human Rights? *They* must know what had really happened, no matter what lies the World Government Police told them.

But how much disturbance had the disappearance of the Fairweather family really made? Maybe it was like dropping a stone into a pond. The ripples would spread out, but in the end they would die away and the pond would be still again. *Out of sight, out of mind,* I remembered as I tidily stacked the clean dishes.

Kristin had gone back to her interrupted meal, tearing the meat off the bone, pushing the scraps into her mouth as if she were afraid of being stopped. Why did she look so strange, so dirty and wild? It was not just the dirt, but a neediness that showed in her tangled hair and filthy clothes, in her hollow cheeks, and in the way her eyes moved constantly, as if a wild beast lurked behind every tree. She was a shocking contrast to the other children, with their clean happy faces and spotless clothes—and their shining confidence.

"What happened to you, Kristin?" I asked abruptly.

"Why aren't you with the others? Your brother, Bobbie—he's here, isn't he?"

Kristin gave a bitter laugh. "Him and his dream of the Big Rock Candy Mountain! Oh yes, kid brother's settled in all right. Got it made." Her voice sounded strident, and I remembered that she'd always been that way with Bobbie, with any small kids who got in her way. Bossy. Almost contemptuous.

"Gordie calls it Xanadu."

"Whatever." She shrugged. "I guess they all have their own name for it. The dream place for kids where there's no interference from the big bad grown-ups."

"Is *that* what this really is? A haven for kids? But where on Earth is this place, Kristin? It's different from anywhere I've ever read about. Almost too good to be real. And how come the police aren't interfering?"

She laughed almost hysterically. "Where on *Earth*? Oh, that's the big question, isn't it, Alison? And too good to be real—that's rich!" Then she stiffened and looked over my shoulder. I turned and saw that the kids were returning from their council.

"I've got to go." She grabbed a piece of bone with meat still hanging from it, and began to run towards the trees that skirted the glade.

"Kristin, wait! We haven't had a real chance to talk. What did you mean by—?"

"Oh, you'll find out soon enough. But Alison, a word of warning, for old times' sake."

"What is it, Kristin?"

"Watch out for that Jay. Don't trust him."

CHAPTER FIVE

I stood staring stupidly at the shadowy trees where Kristin had vanished. Why had she run away? Where had she gone? And what did she mean, *Watch out for that Jay?* Why shouldn't I trust him?

The questions were still whirling around in my head when the children surrounded me.

"Come on. To the fireplace."

"We make a big circle . . ."

". . . and you sit here."

Where was Gordie? I looked anxiously around and glimpsed him among his new-found friends on the far side of the fireplace. For an instant I felt a stab of jealousy. He didn't seem to care at all about what I'd gone through to find him. For all these past months I had been his only friend and teacher. Now, within the space of a day, it seemed he'd turned his back on me and walked happily into a new world with new friends. And a too-good-to-be-true father figure. I didn't matter at all.

I gave myself a mental shake and told myself not to be stupid. Gordie was his own person, and his new independence should make me happy, not jealous. He was safe and that was the important thing. I settled down to pay attention to the story the children had to tell. It came to me in bits and pieces, a sentence from each child, one following another around the circle. They solemnly passed a stick from person to person, and listened to the one holding the stick. When I pieced it all together, their story was like this:

"Here is the Other Place. Here there are no police to be afraid of. This Other Place is all new and the water and air are clean, the way they were in the beginning times. This is the land of the children. It is a gift to us. In return, our gift to the land is to keep it unspoiled forever. And we must be friends. In the Other Place there's no room for quarrelling or being mean."

"We work together," they chorused.

"We talk together and listen to each other. Only when we agree on something do we go ahead and do it."

They stopped and looked expectantly at me as the stick was put into my hand. It was just an ordinary knotted piece of wood, about twenty centimetres long, smoothed with much handling. A zillion questions crowded into my mind, not the least of which was, "But who's really in charge?" The ideals they spoke of were beautiful and worthy, but I had the creepy feeling that the words were being put into their mouths, just as the idea of Xanadu had been put into Gordie's head. As if they were puppets. And who *was* pulling the strings?

Jay, of course, that was obvious—perhaps that was what Kristin had meant when she'd warned me to watch out for him.

I didn't voice any of my suspicions to the kids. "This is a very beautiful place," I said slowly, looking around the circle. "If you can make your community work, you will be building the dream world that humans have been searching for from their very beginnings, way back when they first gathered together around a fire to plan how to trap the mastodons and survive the ice age. But it won't be easy. People have tried and failed before."

"We won't."

"It'll work."

72

"You bet."

I looked around the circle at the eager faces, at the eyes flashing in the dancing flames of the fire, and I decided that I must do my best to protect them from whatever might go wrong in the future—for surely this Other Place was not entirely the paradise it seemed to be. So I had to try to stay close to them, to be part of the group, not an outcast like Kristin. Only then would I have the power to help.

"Have you decided if I am to be part of your community?" I asked quietly and held out the stick.

They looked at one another, their eyes glinting in the firelight. Then one of the older boys took it. "My name is Bryan. I speak for us all. Some of us think that because you're almost grown-up you're bound to want to boss us around—that you just can't help it. The rest of us think you're okay. Gordie here says you've been helping him, teaching him stuff that may be useful for all of us some day. That's good. So long as you don't think that knowing more makes you better. So long as you don't try to run our lives."

I nodded. "Consensus. Cooperation. I can respect those ideas. I do respect them. I'll try to live up to them," I added humbly. And I meant it, even while a part of my brain knew that I was going to investigate this Other Place, and particularly Jay, without asking permission from the group first.

"So we've decided," Bryan went on. "You can stay with us, be part of our group."

"*Our* group." My head jerked up. "Do you mean there are other groups? That you're not alone?"

There was a puzzled silence. After a time Bryan went on uncertainly. "Maybe. Jay will know. You can ask

Jay." Then he added firmly, "But this is *our* group. This is where we stay and work. Look after each other."

"But what about Kristin? You haven't looked after *her*, have you?" Even though the question might endanger my position here, I knew it had to be asked.

I thought they'd look guilty, particularly Bobbie, Kristin's brother, but they didn't. Instead there was a chorus of self-defence.

"She was mean."

"She tried to boss us."

"She made fun of our projects and said we were just little kids. That we couldn't do anything on our own."

"She wouldn't even try to belong."

"But to leave her all alone, outside—wasn't that a mean thing to do?" I asked.

"We always leave meat for her when Jay brings us some." They smiled at each other, confident in their justice.

"Okay. I understand. I've got just one more question—I guess you've thought about it because Gordie has already asked Jay. What should we do about our parents?"

Their looks said as clearly as words: *Why should we worry about* them?

I looked around the circle. "They're still in prison, aren't they? Gordie's and mine certainly are. In the domes. With the sand storm blowing outside and the force field."

They said nothing and I wondered if I was going too far, if I had jeopardized my right to be part of the group.

"You must miss them," I said softly. "I know I do. Maybe not the way they are now," I added, remembering Mom and Dad's total lack of interest in what became of Gordie and me. "But the way they used to be."

There was an uneasy silence. I could see their glances slide from one to another and then away again.

"What's the matter? Are you afraid that you'll get into trouble with the World Police if you help them? But you said there were no police here, didn't you?" *Jay*, I thought. *Maybe, in spite of appearances, they're afraid of Jay*.

"You ask an awful lot of questions, Ally," Bryan said defensively.

"I'm sorry. It's just because I'm new. Because I need to know how things work."

"Can't you just take them the way they are? You're talking like a grown-up."

"I'm sorry. I didn't mean to—"

"Anyway, there aren't any police." A girl of about twelve interrupted me. "Claire and I have been here for ages and we know. The World Police are only in the cities and there aren't any cities here."

"*No cities?*"

They shook their heads. "No cities. No towns either."

"But there must—" I stopped myself. So where did the iron pots and the knives and axe I had seen come from? I decided these were questions I had to save until I could tackle Jay.

I held out my hands, smiled at the group. "Thank you, all of you. I am truly grateful that you're going to allow me to be part of your community. I will do my best to fit in and to help." I spoke formally, and it was obvious that they were pleased.

A girl jumped up and said, "Let's join hands and sing our special song."

"You start the singing, Kate."

She had a true sweet voice. The words were clear,

though simple, and the tune a familiar counting song we'd all learned in school.

"The sky is blue, the sun shines new
On Our Place.
Fruit is sweet, and Jay brings meat
To Our Place.
The water's clean—we'll keep it so,
That trees and grass and all may grow
In Our Place.
We'll all be friends and never fight.
We'll work with love and not through might
To keep this Our Place.
Together one, together all,
We call this—Our Place!"

As I stood with a warm hand clasping each of mine, the sky slowly darkening overhead, I felt closer to this group of unknown children than I had ever felt to anyone in my life before.

The song came to its end, the hands holding mine squeezed gently and were then withdrawn, and the children began to move away.

I ran over to Gordie and gave him a hug. "I'm so happy we both found Xanadu," I whispered.

He nodded and boasted, "I get to sleep in a real cabin." Then he ran to join his new friends.

As I stood, uncertain what I was supposed to do next, Kate, the singer, came up to me with a smile. "You're going to sleep in my cabin, Ally. There's a spare bed."

I followed her towards the trees that surrounded the glade. In the shadows beneath them I could see the outline of half a dozen square mud huts. They were on sloping ground, with their backs dug into the hillside, and since they were roofed with turf, they were almost invisible.

"We girls have these huts, and our latrines are over there." Kate pointed and I went thankfully, though I felt very exposed behind the flimsy roofless structure of thin saplings. Something permanent would certainly be more comfortable, I thought, and wondered if I should suggest it.

"We move them every ten days," Kate explained, answering my unspoken question. "We dig new holes and fill in the old ones. That way they don't get too smelly."

"It must be awfully hard work, digging holes." I wondered how an eager group of eight- to ten-year-olds would manage. Perhaps Jay had "friends" who came in at night to do the heavy work.

"Oh, it's not bad. We all work together, some digging, some loading up the dirt, and others carting it away to dump in the used holes. Working together—that's how we build the cabins too. When I arrived at the Other Place, there were only two cabins. The rest we built as more children came through."

"Came through?" I knew what she meant, but I wondered how *she* remembered the experience.

"Oh, you know. First the dreams. Then voices calling you out of the dome to the Other Place. Then you have to go."

So it had been the same for her as it had been for Gordie. But where did the dreams and the voices come from? Who was responsible? Could this also be the work of the mysterious Jay?

"How long has this been going on?" I asked. "Children coming through, I mean. When did you arrive, for instance?"

"I forget." Kate shrugged. "We don't bother keeping track of days. What's the point?" she added carelessly. "Here we are. This is our cabin."

I could hear the pride in her voice. I looked around. There were no windows and the only illumination came from the open doorway. I wondered if the floor would get wet when it rained. The grass was too green and the trees too lavishly foliaged for this place to have a dry climate. As I grew accustomed to the dim light, I saw that the cabin was simply furnished with three narrow beds, one along each side wall and one across the wall opposite the door. In the space above each there were shelves. The floor was of hardened mud, swept spotlessly clean.

"This is your bed." Kate pointed to the near one on the left side and I sat down cautiously. The "mattress" was made of small springy boughs, covered with a thick pad. A blanket was folded neatly at the bottom, a blanket just like the ones in the dome. Who had brought it here? Jay?

"What about pyjamas?" I asked out loud, and Kate handed me a pair from a pile on one of the shelves. Though they were light blue, rather than the green I was used to, they were in all other respects exactly like the pyjamas I had left behind and obviously from the same source. Whoever was responsible for furnishing the prison habitats had also provided bedding and clothes for the children out here. If the prisons were furnished by the World Government, didn't that mean that the Other Place was also run by them? *By Jay maybe?*

That was my last thought before I fell asleep, soothed by the sound of a soft rain that began to fall as it grew dark. I had grown up with the smell of synthetic walls and floors, furniture and bedding, which after a time became no smell at all. The richness of damp grass and wet earth, the aromatic scents given off by the soft branches on which I lay, were almost overwhelming. Certainly the bed was hard compared with the foam mattress I was accustomed to, but the fresh smell more than made up for that, and I slept soundly and without dreams until the light shining through the doorway woke me.

Still in our pyjamas, and carrying towels and clean overalls, the three of us, Kate, Alicia and I, took a narrow path to where a stream flowed down the hillside. There we met the other girls and I followed their lead and jumped into the water. Cold! I yelled out loud and found myself, just for a second, regretting the bathroom in the dome. But here we weren't limited to a one-minute shower. We splashed each other, laughed and played, and before long I didn't notice the coldness of the water any more. We rubbed our bodies and hair with an aromatic jelly that foamed like soap and left my body tingling and my hair soft and sweet-smelling.

"We make it from the leaves of a bush, boiled and then strained," Claire explained. "There are no bad chemicals in it to hurt the water."

"It's just wonderful. How did you find out about it?" I was met with blank looks.

"We've always used it" was the answer.

I was given a pair of fresh overalls to wear while my green ones were washed and hung over a bush to dry in the sun. They fit fairly well, though they were too short in the legs and sleeves. Obviously my arrival had not been counted on or catered to. I wondered if someone out there would see to it that there were overalls to fit me within the next few days.

Shoes were not a problem, since no one wore them. That made sense, I realized, since foot sizes varied enormously, and children's feet grow quickly. As I hobbled up the stony path, I guessed that the hardest part of getting used to the Other Place might be toughening up the soles of my feet.

After breakfast we brushed the cabin floor—it was bone dry, no rain had come in—and put our blankets and mattress pads out to air on the bushes outside. Then the group decided that it was time to build another cabin, since the boys' cabins were all filled up after Gordie's arrival.

With intervals for meals this work took three days. There was the sod to cut and set aside, to be used later for the roof. Then we had to level off the floor by digging back into the hillside and removing the dirt. Another group cut saplings for the walls and the roof. My height turned out to be very useful for putting the upper walls and roofing into place, but I was always careful not to push myself forward, waiting instead until I was asked to help. I noticed that there was something for everyone to do. Even the smallest ones happily worked clay and water into a thick paste that was then pushed in between the saplings to make the walls and roof weather-proof.

I was glad I held back. By waiting and watching I learned just how resourceful the children were. Often the solution to some problem would come from the very youngest children, whose imaginations for the "possible" were least restricted. And sixty hands, even small ones, could accomplish a great deal when they worked together.

I began to understand how clever the designer of this community was. Every child had a purpose. Nobody was left out or belittled. I could see in their shining faces the reward for their hard work when, in three days, the new cabin was finished. The mud floor and chinking in the walls were barely dry when a new child came through and was proudly introduced to his new home. "We all made the cabin Matthew," Bryan said. "And we'll teach you so you can help too."

Apparently Gordie had boasted about my teaching ability, but there seemed to be little I could offer that the children were interested in. Some simple addition and multiplication—how many saplings would it take to build a new hut? How many roots were enough for dinner? This was useful. Storytelling and poetry were a big hit, especially the poem about Xanadu, but they were better at making up working and counting songs than I was. As for geography, since we didn't know where on Earth we were, what was the point? And as for history—forget it! The children weren't interested in the past, only the future. *Their* future.

For my own interest I began to make an inventory of all the plants that grew within walking distance of our village. Some of these were already in use, such as the bushes that supplied soap for both dishes and personal use, and the trees whose rough, dense leaves gave us scrubbing cloths. But I began to discover other unknown plants and brought them back to the village in a bag of grass I had braided myself. Before long I noticed that Alicia and Kate and some of the others were copying my design, and soon they were producing little bags of their own.

I tested the plants I picked, boiling them to extract the

juice from leaves and roots or drying them like herbs. I tried them out first on myself, and only a few caused minor problems: one made me sick and another gave me a mild skin rash. Soon we had tasty herbs and roots to add to the vegetable stew, and I discovered some interesting dyes—if only we had cloth to dye.

I wished I still had my diary, not only to jot down daily happenings and my feelings, but also to make lists of my various discoveries. One day, perhaps, I might have time to find substitutes for paper and pen, but for now I was too busy. *I must keep my findings in my memory*, I told myself, and I discovered that, indeed, my memory sharpened with practice.

At first my explorations were limited to the area immediately around our glade. I remember the first time I unthinkingly walked until I was completely lost. I turned around to see nothing but trees and more trees. Which way was home? My whole life had been bounded by a crosshatch of numbered streets and avenues, where it was really not possible to get lost.

I remember turning and turning again in a panic until the tree trunks became like the bars of another kind of prison. My mouth got dry and I could feel my heart beating faster and faster. Then Matthew and Gordie ran by giggling, chasing some small furry creature that scurried into the underbrush. Gordie was rosy-cheeked and happy, and—no longer lost—I was doubly delighted to see him.

"Hi, Ally, what're you doing?"

I swallowed and steadied my voice. "Just on my way back," I lied. "Want to carry my bag?"

"Sure."

They made off unerringly in a direction that seemed

to me exactly like every other direction, and within a short time the glade was in sight.

"Gordie, how did you know this was the way back?"

He stared at me as if I was crazy. "'Cause it was."

"How about you, Matthew? You've only been here a short while. How did you know?"

He thought about it. "Uphill's away. And downhill's back, I guess."

I blinked at the obviousness of it. "But suppose you go over the top of the hill and down into another glade— like this one, only different—would you be lost?"

"Maybe." He shrugged and looked at Gordie for support.

"We don't go far, Ally. Just around here. Kate and Bryan—they know more, I think. I'd go with them if I wanted to explore far away."

"But why would you want to, Gordie? Here's so neat." Matthew looked around the glade at the bustling children, at the fire burning cheerfully in the centre.

I knew what he meant, but I was determined to explore farther. I decided to stick to the small trails left by passing animals, and to mark my way in some fashion so that I wouldn't get lost. *A compass would be really helpful*, I thought, but there was no compass. *The position of the sun should help, then.* I would have to learn to pay attention to details like that.

Once the others understood the usefulness of what I was doing, I was often given afternoons to myself. As I became familiar with the countryside and was no longer afraid of losing my way, I began to explore farther afield. I tried, on some of these excursions, to find my way back to the place where I had broken through the force field around the dome, but I was never able to find it. Nor was I able to find the way to any of the other domes, even though there must have been thirty or so scattered around the countryside. I wondered why I could never find one, and why I never smelled the ozone or stumbled into an area of high electrical output. Perhaps one of the functions of the force fields was to bend light waves in such a way that a person automatically walked around them, as if they weren't there at all. True invisibility.

At the back of my mind was a plan to find Kristin and talk to her again. I had seen her only briefly on the occasions when Jay brought us a beast to roast. Each time a platter of scraps was left for her, and she appeared from among the trees, ate greedily and vanished again before I had a chance to talk privately to her.

In the end it was my sense of smell, sharpened in this place of many exotic scents, that led me to her hiding place. It was the smell of unwashed hair and body, of grime and grease. I followed it, stopping to sniff, catching the trail again and walking softly on my newly hardened feet.

I found her in a kind of natural cave formed where an ancient and giant tree had fallen and pulled away part of the bank on which it had grown. She had lined the cavity with torn-up grass, and she was curled up in it, sound asleep, like an animal in its lair. She looked and smelled somewhat like an animal too, her skin grimy and her hair a tangled mat. *How could an achiever like Kristin sink so low?* I asked myself.

Now wait a minute, Alison, an inner voice reproved me. *How would you react to being alone in a strange country with no friends, nowhere to sleep and no tools to make a house?*

By the time she stirred, I had become ashamed of my thoughts and was totally in sympathy with her. When her eyes opened and she saw me sitting there, she made as if to leap up and run, and I had to grab her arm to hold her back. She saw who it was and relaxed.

"Oh, it's you. Come to gloat, have you?"

My sympathy lessened a bit. "Don't be stupid, Kristin. I've come to help, if you'll let me."

"A scrap of leftover dinner, perhaps?"

"Of course not. But I did bring a snack with me, and you're welcome to share it if you'd like." I rummaged in the grass bag I used to carry specimens, and pulled out some fruit and a piece of flatbread. This bread was a new experiment of mine. I had painstakingly made flour by grinding between two stones the seeds of a local grass rather like rye, and then had baked the dough on hot stones beside the fire.

She grabbed the bread, tore off a hunk and stuffed it in her mouth. "Not bad," she mumbled. "Don't bother with fruit. There's plenty of that for the picking. But it doesn't fill one up like meat or bread." She scratched her arm as she chewed. I noticed it was inflamed and swollen.

"There's a leaf that makes a kind of soap. There's plenty of it around here, I've noticed. You'd be better off getting cleaned up. And we use it for shampoo too."

"Forget it," she said. "If it doesn't bother me, it shouldn't bother you."

"It's no problem," I couldn't help retorting, "so long as I can sit upwind of you."

She flushed at that and looked at the leaves I'd been collecting. "Like these? How do you use them?"

"Just boil them for a while and then strain off the liquid."

She shrugged. "There you are then. I haven't got a lighter or matches. How can I make a fire?"

"But that's awful!" I thought again of what her life alone must be like. "Kristin, have you talked to Jay? He should at least see that you've got matches and a good knife and an axe. What's going to become of you when it gets cold?"

"If it does."

"It's bound to. All the vegetation indicates that this is a temperate climate. Sooner or later there's going to be a winter, however short and mild. You *have* to have shelter and fire and a decent diet. Otherwise you'd be better off back in your dome."

"Don't I know it. I've looked for the way back, but I can't find it. Not anywhere. I wish he *would* send me back."

"Could he do that? How?"

She stared. "Come on, Ally! It's perfectly obvious he's in charge. He calls the little kids over, doesn't he?"

"Someone does," I admitted and then remembered. "He was waiting for me when I came through."

"Me too. That first day it all looked so good." She sighed. "Then he let my creepy brother Bobbie influence the others to throw me out. You'd think he would have interfered, wouldn't you? But oh no. He let them get away with it."

"Have you ever asked if you could join the others? Have you ever said you'd go along with their ideas and not fight them?"

"Are you nuts?"

"Better a slice of humble pie than living like a dog," I said crossly and got to my feet. Kristin had been my best friend, but now I found myself wondering why.

She'd always been bossy and hard to get on with if she didn't get her way. I guess I'd got in the habit of letting her have it.

"Don't go. I didn't mean to snap." She grabbed my arm. "Stay a bit longer."

"It's almost time for supper. The kids'll wonder where I've got to."

"You will come back, won't you?"

"Sure, if you want me to." I tried not to show my surprise. I thought she'd never want to see me again. "I'll bring that shampoo for you, if you like," I offered.

"You might as well," she said grudgingly.

"I'll talk to Jay too, if I can get hold of him. He's not often around."

"Ally, have you ever wondered where he goes when he's not in the village? He doesn't sleep there, does he?"

"No, he doesn't. I thought maybe there was a town close by, but the kids say there isn't."

Her dirty face creased into a humourless smile. "A town? Really, Alison, how dumb can you get!"

I turned away, irritated. "I do have to go. I don't want to be caught away from the village when it starts to get dark."

"You've never been out at night, have you?"

I shook my head. "We're always in bed and asleep by dusk."

"You should stay awake one night and look around. You might be surprised."

Her enigmatic words made no sense to me, so I shrugged, grabbed my plaited bag and jogged as quickly as I could back to the village. Luckily it hadn't been my turn to help cook dinner, and I was able to store my herbs and be at the table in time for the meal.

I hoped I would have a chance to talk to Jay, but he was nowhere around. *Where does he go?* I asked myself. He couldn't be camping out. He was always dapper and clean shaven, with his strange costume unrumpled and unstained. I still thought that somewhere close by there must be a town, despite Kristin's sneers. What did *she* know about it?

Thinking of Kristin reminded me of her suggestion that I go outdoors at night. Comfortable and well-fed, I found I normally slid into sleep as soon as I put my head down in the quiet twilight of the cabin, and nothing woke me until the morning sun shone on my face.

But my curiosity was aroused and I was sure I could stay awake if I chose to. Instead of curling up comfortably under my blanket, I lay straight on my back and stared at the oblong of light that marked the doorway. It seemed to take forever for the light to fade away completely, so that I could no longer distinguish the doorway from the darkness inside the room. Finally I judged it was dark enough and slid quietly out of bed. Neither Kate nor Alicia stirred as I crept towards the door.

I threaded my way between the shadowy trees to the open glade. Above my head the stars blazed. Beautiful, but unrecognizable. Back in the city the grimy skies and the lurid laser displays from nightclubs and advertisements always hid the night sky from us, so my only experience of stars had been through viddisks and a school visit to a planetarium.

"You might be surprised," Kristin had said enigmatically. I yawned and shivered slightly as the cool breeze flapped the legs of my pyjamas. *She's a little crazy, after all,* I told myself. *Living alone. Eating badly. It's not surprising.* I was about to return to my warm bed when the moon appeared above the trees. I stared at it, blinked and rubbed my eyes.

The moon was full and the glade should have been brightly lit, I knew, even though my experience of the night sky was limited. Large, yellowish white, with a smiling face—that was the moon I knew. But I saw no familiar smile. This moon was small and dimmer than I had expected.

We're somewhere in the southern hemisphere, I told myself firmly. *A place where everything is upside down and the sun shines in the north.* I had just about convinced myself that this was so when the impossible happened. A *second* moon popped up above the trees. It was larger and brighter than the first and had shadowy markings on it, but none that resembled the familiar man-in-the-moon image.

As I stood watching the two discs, the second crept closer to the first. I stared, oblivious of the cool wind flapping at my pyjamas. If I were to wait long enough, I realized, the newcomer would overtake the other, eclipse it and move on in its orbit through the alien sky. I did not wait but turned away, stumbled across the glade and ran through the trees to our cabin.

Back in bed I pulled the blanket over my head and crouched there, shivering spasmodically. My body warmed up at last, but the shivering didn't go away. I lay in the darkness trying to struggle with the dreadful fact that Gordie and I, Mom and Dad, in fact all the disappeareds were truly exiled and were never, ever, going to go home. We were too far away. In an alien world. Out of sight, out of mind.

Gordie's Xanadu—the Other Place—was an alien

planet, orbiting a foreign sun and circled by two foreign moons. I found myself recalling an earlier conversation with Kristin. "Where on Earth are we?" I'd asked. And she had laughed.

Now I knew why she'd laughed. We weren't on Earth. We were Nowhere.

CHAPTER SIX

I must have slept in snatches during that long night because Kate had to shake me awake in the morning, but my memory is of hour after long hour of wakeful speculation. *How did we get here? Where is here? Why hadn't any rumour of what was really happening to the disappeareds ever leaked out? How could a secret this huge be kept for so long?*

Ms. MacKenzie's voice echoed in my head. "Long ago, over three hundred years ago, people guilty of no more than stealing a loaf of bread were transported to Australia—to that 'far shore', as it came to be called."

"Abandoned?" someone had asked. Was it Kristin?

"Not quite as bad as that. Ships did call at Australian ports. People who were not convicts eventually came to live there. And the ships sailed back home to England—there was always that possibility of two-way travel when a convict's sentence was completed."

Not like us, I thought bitterly. *We are stuck here for life, somewhere out in the galaxy, in a place we don't even know the name of.*

One-way traffic. Though I had never seen or even heard the sound of a ferry landing here from an interstellar spaceship, new disappeareds continued to arrive. The domes had been outfitted with Earth furnishings, and the occupants ate Earth food. The force fields were Earth technology. It had to mean that someone from the World Police was running the show—was in charge. Who could it be? Was that person here, in Xanadu? Policeman Jay.

He knew we were on another planet. He knew, but he hadn't told us.

Kristin knew the significance of the two moons. And she had warned me to look out for Jay. In her solitary days she must have done a lot of thinking about our situation. *I've got to talk to her. Later today I'll slip away,* I promised myself.

But my plans didn't work out as I'd hoped.

"Ten days since we dug new latrines," Bryan reminded us after breakfast. There was a general groan, but everyone agreed that indeed new latrines were necessary. The decision was made and there was no way I could leave. My private plans had to be put on hold as Tomas, Bryan and I, the oldest and strongest, were picked to do the heavy digging.

The group was wonderfully organized. The young ones peeled away the turf from the new sites and set it aside. There were six latrines, so that meant each of us had to dig two holes apiece, about a metre square and two metres deep. The work wasn't too tough at first, and we had good spades—Earth technology again, I reminded myself.

But once I was below ground and found my movements restricted by the walls of the pit, it grew more difficult. Instead of digging and throwing the dirt aside, I was forced to loosen the soil, patch by patch, and scrape it into baskets that the younger ones then hauled up to the surface and carried away to fill in the used pits.

With three holes half-dug we stopped and ate our lunch of fruit and flatbread, standing around, dirty and sweaty, groaning and holding our tired backs. But by the end of the afternoon there were three fresh latrines, with clean-scrubbed seats and screens of saplings, and the old pits had been filled in and turfed over.

As I crouched in the cool stream, letting the dirt and sweat wash away, I felt tired but somehow fulfilled, and that night, in spite of my worries and questions, I fell asleep as soon as my eyes closed.

On the morning of the next day Jay dropped off a small buck-like creature already dressed for roasting, and two of the smallest children were at once put to the job of turning the spit and watching that the meat didn't burn. I thought quickly of challenging him there and then, before talking to Kristin, but the choice was taken out of my hands. Jay didn't stay, but vanished among the trees like a shadow.

The encouraging smell of cooking meat wafted across to us as we dug the last three pits, and the promise of a feast encouraged us to get the work done even more quickly. We laughed and splashed each other as we cleaned ourselves afterwards, and put on fresh overalls to celebrate.

I felt suddenly very happy. Why? What was different? Then I realized that it was because I was now part of the group, that I was family. What magic Jay had wrought, bringing us together like this! Surely he couldn't be bad—or not all bad. Not World Police.

These youngsters were closer to me than Mom and Dad had ever been. I respected every one of the children, from Bryan down to the smallest, Alicia and Merry. And they respected me. Only when we sat down to share the feast did a shadow cross this shining landscape. I looked up and there was Kristin, suddenly appearing among the trees, wild, dirty and waif-like. For a moment I saw her not as my old school friend, but as a stranger, an outcast. One who didn't belong. The way the others did.

But aren't we all outcasts in this Other Place? I asked myself. I slipped quietly away from the table and quickly put into one of my grass collecting bags a small pot of soap, a towel and my old green overalls—I had indeed been supplied with ones that fit. I walked to a big tree on the far side of the glade, close to the path down which Kristin had come, and I casually dropped the bag. No one seemed to notice as I came back to the table and helped the others clear.

The next afternoon I was finally able to get away. With my collecting bag slung over my shoulder I set off up the hill towards Kristin's lair. I hoped that my gifts had not been taken as criticism and that I'd find her in a more receptive mood than the previous time we'd met.

I had also slipped a fresh disc of flatbread into my bag. This was definitely not a cooperative act and I felt a bit guilty, but I told myself that, after all, it was I who had discovered the breadgrass and spent hours experimenting, grinding the seeds, mixing the flour with water and some sweet tree sap, and baking the dough on hot stones until I got it right.

It was a beautiful day, the sun shining brightly through the shade trees. Indeed, the days were always beautiful, and it seemed to rain only at night. Normally I would have enjoyed the walk, smelling the incense trees, the honey scent of some flowering creeper, the moist earth under old leaves, and listening to birdsong and the music of small streams cascading down the hillside.

But today my mood was all wrong. I found myself criticizing the perfection. In how many places does it rain only at night? In how many countries are there *no* unpleasant insects or venomous snakes? The only wildlife I ever saw were birds, and the occasional small furry mammals rustling among the fallen leaves and scampering along the trails. Where were the big beasts that Jay brought for our feasts? If I were suddenly to meet up with one, would it be dangerous? Somehow I was sure that I never would, because a threatening animal would spoil the idea of paradise, of Xanadu. I stopped suddenly on the shady path as a new thought flashed into my mind. *It is all too beautiful to be true.*

When I reached the uprooted tree, Kristin wasn't there, but she had left a wet towel hanging over a bush to dry. I sat down to wait for her, and before long she appeared from among the trees, dressed in my old green overalls, her face shining with cleanness and her hair in a bright cloud around her head.

"A comb would have been useful" was her greeting, and all the thanks I was to get. Obviously she was as prickly as ever.

I managed a smile and said smoothly, not showing my irritation, "Sorry about that. But there are only a few wooden combs in the village and it wouldn't have been fair to take one. But you look fantastic anyway."

She gave a sarcastic laugh. "Not fair? Cooperation and consensus, I suppose? You *have* bought the party line, haven't you? What happened to the old idea of 'each woman for herself'?"

"That was never my ideal, Kristin," I snapped. "And I think this community's got a great deal going for it. Maybe they'll have a better chance here than back on—" I stopped abruptly. Somehow, between that awful night of the discovery of the two moons and now, I had come to terms with our situation. Perhaps digging those latrines had done the trick.

"You were going to say 'back on Earth', weren't you? So you know. You went out at night?"

"Yes. And I know. But I don't understand. Why are we here? How did we get here? And where *is* here?"

"There's only one person on the planet who knows the answers to all those questions."

"And that's Jay." I nodded. "That's why I came. We've got to get him alone and tackle him. But he's slippery and hard to pin down."

"Impossible, I'd say. He'll only hang around if *he* wants to talk to *you*. No, I've got a better idea." She squatted on the tree trunk beside me. "Got any more of that bread?"

I pulled the disc from my bag and handed it over. She grabbed at it, tore off a piece and stuffed it in her mouth.

"What we should do," she said indistinctly, "is follow him."

"Follow Jay? But where?"

"Wherever he goes. He always takes the same path when he leaves the village. I've hidden and watched him. He must have some kind of camp or hide-out, and I think it'll be worth our while to follow him and find out where it is. I've thought of doing it before, but not alone. I don't trust him. Now that you're here, it's different. I can count on you, Ally, can't I?"

I nodded. "Of course. But it's not always easy to get away. How long do you think it'll take us?"

Kristin shrugged. "Who's to say? Sometimes I don't see him for days. But always when he's been hunting, he goes by this way to the village. And on the way back, he always takes the same path."

"I can't stay here on the off-chance that he'll be by. I'll be missed and the others will ask questions. Jay's bound to find out and then he'll get suspicious."

"No, I can see that wouldn't work. My idea is that you keep a lookout, and as soon as you see Jay delivering the next beast, get up here as fast as you can. I'll be waiting. Then, as soon as he goes by on his way to wherever he goes, we'll follow him. You won't be missed for a while, and the kids will just think you're on one of your botanical expeditions."

"That sounds good. He usually brings a beast twice in every ten-day. He came yesterday, so four days from now . . ."

"That'll give you time to bake extra flatbread for the journey. We don't know how far we'll have to go. We'd better be prepared."

I nodded. "And I'd better go now, so that I'm back in time for supper."

"Don't let me down, Ally."

"Of course not. Who do you think I am? We're best friends, aren't we, Kristin?"

She stared at me and I could almost hear her saying, "You're so naive, Alison." Then she shrugged and what she said was, "We *were*. But that's a long time ago and *very* far away."

With those words she pushed me away, so I picked up my bag and began to walk down towards the village without another word. I didn't look back, though I had the feeling that she was watching me go. What was there to say? In Xanadu she was an outcast and I was "in". It had changed our relationship completely and I wasn't sure how to handle it.

Autumn was coming, if there was such a season as autumn in this world. At any rate the nuts were ripening on the trees and beginning to fall to the ground. We gathered them and dried them until we could pull off their leathery outer husks, and then we stored them.

Besides the cabins the village also had a storage hut, distinguished from the rest by the fact that it had a door. We kept it tightly closed to discourage any marauding animals from making off with the growing store of ripe nuts, dried fruit and the sacks of breadgrass grain that I encouraged the younger ones to collect.

What would winter be like? Our clothing was light syncot. The cabins had no doors to keep out the cold. Our dinner table sat under the open sky, so that every meal was a picnic. There was no community building where we might gather in bad weather. Perhaps "winter" was just a word for a time when there was no fresh fruit. I certainly hoped so.

This gathering of nuts and drying of fruit seemed to have started spontaneously in the community—but I doubted this. I believed that in some way Jay had planted the idea of a coming winter in the heads of some of the older children, Bryan perhaps, and Kate and Tomas, but because of the nightly discussions and consensus, it was hard to tell where an idea actually began. Except for the flatbread—that invention had been all mine. Then I had the creepy idea that perhaps I hadn't thought of it, that perhaps Jay had in some way also planted it in my head. Could he get inside our brains? Was he the puppet-master pulling our strings?

During the next four days, besides gathering nuts and berries with the group, I spent my spare moments grinding more breadgrass into flour and baking flatbreads. For every five discs I piled on the shelf in the storeroom I secreted another away in my grass bag, which I kept on the shelf above my bed.

On the fifth day I managed to get myself assigned to lighting and tending the big fire. The community had several tinderboxes with which we could laboriously make a spark. These were small metal boxes with tight waterproof lids, each containing a piece of flint and a small steel rod. The rest of the box was filled with dry moss, bark, or anything else that would ignite easily and start a fire.

I wondered why Jay had provided flint and steel when he could as easily have given the community a supply of lighters or even old-fashioned matches. Perhaps he had some idea of making us self-sufficient, which was good as far as it went. But then where did the flint come from? Was he going to tell us one day? As it was, the tinderboxes seemed to me an elaborate nuisance, and I was much less successful at starting a fire than even the smallest of the children.

This morning, once the fire was going well, I concentrated on feeding it from a nearby pile of dead wood while keeping an eye on that part of the glade in which Jay usually appeared. As soon as I saw the fluttering blue-black of his garments, I passed my duty on to one of the younger ones, ran back to my cabin, grabbed my bag of provisions and then headed up the hill into the trees.

I ran from tree to tree, circling the glade, until I reached the place where Jay had arrived. Then I climbed briskly up to the ridge and Kristin's fallen tree.

She was already waiting for me, and without a word of greeting she set off at a fast pace up the ridge, not stopping until we came to a stony outcrop that over-hung the valley to our left. There we waited in silence while I thought irritably, *Suppose Jay stays in the village? If I were there I'd have a chance to talk to him instead of wasting my time sitting here.*

Once a faint rustle in the bushes alerted us, but it was only a small creature with greenish fur. It trotted by, ignoring us completely, and scampered into the under-growth. We tried to relax again, silently watching the faint trail that Jay would follow.

At last we heard the crack of a dry branch below us and there was Jay, walking briskly along as if he were going somewhere definite—such as home. We gave him a little time to get past us and then followed him, stay-ing high on the ridge above his path.

Soon we were farther away from the village and the familiar hills surrounding it than I had ever ventured. I had brought the knife I normally used to cut any woody plants I wanted to collect, and now and then I marked a blaze at eye level on the far side of trees so that we might not lose our way on our return. Perhaps I could trust Kristin to find her way back, but I wanted to be doubly sure.

We had been climbing steadily ever since we had set out, and the track below, along which Jay strode, also led upwards. The stream beside the trail became smaller until it was only a trickle and finally vanished altogether.

At last we reached the summit and stood gasping, not just from the exertion of our climb but at the breath-taking view that met our eyes. Across the far landscape stretched a vista of distant purple mountains. Closer to hand dense dark forests carpeted the land right up to the base of the cliffs where we stood. The near ground fell abruptly away beneath us in tier after tier of craggy rock. Down this gorge Jay's path zigzagged to and fro in a series of switchbacks. A stream cascaded down beside it, and heavy mist hid the bottom of the valley from our eyes.

Suddenly the sun came out from behind a cloud and the air between us and the misty valley was filled with a brilliant arc of rainbow. As we stood enthralled by the sight, almost forgetting why we were there, we became aware of a low, ceaseless roaring sound, like a strong wind. It was obviously safe to talk. Ahead of us Jay could not possibly hear.

"We've got to get down to the trail." Kristin pointed.

"I hope he doesn't see us. We'll be close behind him then."

"It's a risk we'll have to take. No reason why he should turn round."

Clinging to the trunks of trees and the whippy branches of small bushes, our bare toes digging into the meagre soil, we slithered and scrambled down the steep slope from the ridge to the track below. By the time we had set our feet on the relatively level path, Jay was well out of sight.

We walked as quickly as we could, but our pace soon slowed to a crawl when the path changed from one wide enough for us to walk side by side to little more than a ledge, with the cliff rising rockily on one side and the gorge plunging to unguessable depths on the other. Each time we came to a curve or a bulge in the rock that hid the way ahead, we had to slow down even more in case Jay should be there, right in front of us. But we never saw him. It was almost as if he'd sprouted wings and flown down the gorge.

We had set out soon after breakfast, and it was afternoon before we finally reached a plateau halfway down the cliff. It was a fearsome sight, for the stream, cascading down the gorge in a series of wild waterfalls on our left, now plummeted abruptly into a cavern that opened up in the cliff like a huge gaping mouth. The sound of its fall was an enormous continuous thunder, and the air was filled with a dense mist that obscured our view.

Once we ventured a little closer, we could see that the cave walls had been polished by the continuous passage of water as the river curled over the edge into the abyss in a smooth and glassy curve, flecked with swirling foam. I found myself being drawn closer and closer to the edge, as if the falling water were pulling me hypnotically towards itself. Kristin broke the spell by grabbing my arm and pulling me back. My knees gave way and I collapsed, shuddering, onto a rock running with moisture. What a terrifying place!

"There's no sign of Jay." Kristin was matter-of-fact, unmoved by the tumult of the waters. "Where could he have gone?"

I shook my head to clear my brain, dizzied by the sight and sound. Jay? I had almost forgotten that he was the reason we were here. I looked around. The cliff rose sheer above our heads to the left. At our feet the river fell into the dark cavern. To our right, far below, the bottom of the gorge was carpeted in what seemed to be impenetrable forest. So where was Jay? How had he vanished? By magic? In this awesome place I could easily believe in magic.

As my fear of the depths and the falling water slowly subsided, I began to realize how tired I was. My legs ached and my hands shook with fatigue. I was also ravenously hungry. "Aren't you starving, Kristin? We'd better have something to eat before we decide what to do."

She shrugged. "I guess I am. I hadn't noticed."

I felt myself burning with shame at the realization that hunger was probably Kristin's familiar companion, that to her there was nothing unusual in the pain of an empty stomach. I, on the other hand, had been spoiled with three good meals a day.

I unslung my bag from across my shoulder, passed her a disc of flatbread and broke one for myself. We ate in silence. The noise of the cascading water was too great for ordinary conversation. When our meal of bread, fruit and a handful of nuts was finished, we drank handfuls of icy water from the falls.

The commonplace acts of eating bread and drinking water had steadied my jangling nerves, and I got up from my rocky seat and looked around. Jay could not have simply vanished. There had to be a logical explanation for his disappearance.

"There's something over there, on the wall of the cave." I pointed. "Do you see? It looks almost like a vine. But how could a vine grow down there in the dark?"

Kristin followed the direction of my pointing finger. "Let's look." She jumped to her feet and fearlessly approached the edge, her feet only centimetres away from the glassy downward curve of the water.

I shuddered. "Kristin, be careful."

"I'm fine, Ally. Grab my hand. I want to get a closer look."

I hung on to her hand as she leaned precariously forward. "It's a rope, fastened to the wall," she said breathlessly. "It follows the waterfall down. So this is where Jay's gone. Underground!"

Once accustomed to the dim light under the cover of the overhanging rock, I too could see the synfibre rope leading downwards into the dark. It was fastened to the rock wall with metal rings that gleamed wetly in the deluge of spray.

"Now at last we're going to find out Jay's secrets!" Kristin gloated. Perhaps she wasn't frightened the way I was because she had so little to lose. Or maybe I was just a coward. I could feel myself drawing back. Was it worth risking our lives just to find out what Jay was up to? I knew I couldn't abandon Kristin now—I'd given her my promise. But nothing was going to persuade me to go down into that darkness.

"How can we possibly find our way without a torch?" I hedged.

"Didn't you bring anything with you?"

"I wasn't expecting— No, wait a minute." I remembered the tinderbox I'd used to start the fire that morning. I patted my overall pocket. "Yes, here it is. So all we need is a dry branch, if we can find such a thing in all this deluge."

I thankfully backed away from the dizzying waterfall and searched the edge of the plateau until I found the partly broken-off branch of an incense tree. I was able to cut it free with my knife, and even though the wood was damp I could see fresh gum oozing from the cut end. I struck flint against steel, managed to ignite the dry bark I carried in the tinderbox with the spark, and shielding it with my body from the ever-present spray, lit the sappy end of the branch. It burst at once into flame and burned with a clear bright light and a sweet perfume. I slipped the tinderbox into my bag, which I decided to leave tucked behind a handy rock.

"There's nothing to stop us now," Kristin said triumphantly, and I realized that it wasn't just curiosity that was pitting her against Jay, but vengeance. She had a score to settle, and her anger would take her recklessly into places where I was afraid to venture. I told myself that I couldn't possibly follow her down that awful chute with nothing but a frail rope between me and certain death. I would wait for her at the top.

But she grabbed the rope and took the first step, looking back over her shoulder. "Come on, Ally. Hurry. Hold up that torch."

So weakly I gave in, swallowed my panic and followed her, the torch held high in my left hand, my right hand gripping the rope. As the flame flickered over the streaming walls, I could see just how precarious our descent was going to be. We were creeping down a roughly carved set of stairs, crooked and uneven, running with water, so that every step was an invitation to disaster. It would only take one slip. No human being could possibly survive the fall down that horrible chute. If we fell we would be either drowned or battered to death somewhere in the blackness at the bottom.

"I can't go on, Kristin!" I yelled, but the rushing water must have swallowed my words because she paid no heed and continued climbing downwards.

I crept down behind her, step by dizzy step, ever deeper into the earth, clinging desperately to the rope, the torch flickering wildly above my head. The air grew steadily colder and I was drenched to the skin. Worse than the discomfort of cold seeping through my wet overalls was the fact that my feet had become numb. I could no longer feel each slippery step. At one point my bare toes caught on a small ridge of rock and I stumbled forward and nearly fell. I clung to the rope and torch, and tried to calm my ragged breathing.

"You all right, Ally?"

All right? I felt like saying. *No, Kristin, I'm going to die.*

"Sure. How much farther, do you think?" I forced the words out through my chattering teeth.

"I see something ahead. A light. Could it be a light?"

"Jay?"

"I can't imagine that he's that close. Oh, Ally, look! We've made it!"

The torch showed us a side passage, mercifully dry and running straight and level. The walls and floor had been laser-smoothed, and the ceiling was set with light panels.

Safely inside, I collapsed on the floor and began to massage my numb feet, moaning as the feeling came back into my toes. *I'll have some great bruises in the morning,* I thought. *If I survive that long.*

"The torch is pretty useless now. Give it here." Kristin took it from me and went back to extinguish its flame in the falling water.

"This is all Earth technology," I pointed out when she returned. Away from the roar of the waterfall the quiet was almost deafening, and we found ourselves talking in whispers. "These natural tunnels have been laser-smoothed. And those lights . . ." I stared up at her. "You don't seem surprised."

She shook her head. "I was always sure the World Government was involved in this. After all, the prisons are WOGPO. So is the diet and our clothing."

"But listen, Kristin. The children are on their own. They have to build their shelter, gather their own food—"

"Except for the meat Jay provides."

"But it's real meat, not syntho— not Earth made."

"Nevertheless I think the children are being trained, and who by but WOGPO?"

"What for?" I challenged.

Kristin shrugged. "That's what we hope to find out. How are your feet now?" She sounded impatient.

"Fine." I scrambled up. In fact my toes were throbbing furiously, but I limped on, trying to keep up with her long strides.

We made good time along the smooth-floored passageway for a while. Then we came to an intersection. "Right or left?"

"Let's take alternate rights and lefts. Less likely to go in circles."

We picked right and went on. At the next intersection we turned left. But there were dead-ends and double choices, and before long I was convinced we were completely lost and wondered how we would ever find our way back to the surface. As we stood hesitating at yet another branch in the passageway, we heard a faint tuneful hum, amplified by the tunnels around us.

I grabbed Kristin and pulled her back into the passage we had just left. We stood as flat as we could against the bare wall, trying to make ourselves invisible. The humming grew louder. I held my breath and tightened my muscles so that not a tremor or the flicker of an eyelid could betray my presence.

I saw a dancing shadow on the polished floor of the passage we had been about to enter. It shortened and vanished. For a brief second the blue and black motley of Jay's costume flashed by. Then the shadow appeared behind him, lengthened and vanished. We stood frozen for what felt like forever.

"He must be out of earshot by now," I whispered at last.

"Wow, that was close! At least now we know which way to go. Come on." Kristin bounded off down the passage from which Jay had emerged. There were no more side tunnels. Before long the rock walls abruptly widened into a huge space, a brilliantly lit room, silent except for the whisper of an air conditioner.

"Look at all this computer equipment!" I exclaimed, staring at the banks of consoles and vidscreens, all the technological paraphernalia of the world we had left behind.

"And what about those monitors?" Kristin pointed to the end of the room where thirty screens were mounted on the wall in a double row. Each bore a letter of the alphabet—from A to Z, plus AA to DD.

"The habitats," I guessed. "So we *were* being spied on all the time. By *Jay*." I sat down at the main computer, switched on and accessed program files. There it was: HABITATS. I clicked on, entered "W" and there, on the appropriate screen, was my familiar prison. The camera—how come I had never noticed a camera?—was aimed at the wall, where one of Mom's murals suddenly appeared, a weird abstraction in purple and green.

"Where are you, Mom?" I moved the mouse and the camera swung dizzily to a glimpse of her arm. I moved it again and felt a sudden pang of— What was it? Homesickness? Nostalgia? Surely not. For there she was, hair a bird's nest, clothes untidy, but perfectly happy and well, as far as I could tell. Her lips moved and I guessed she was singing to herself as she splashed on the paint.

I wished I could talk to her. Tell her that Gordie and I were okay. That we'd try to get her out—if she wanted out. *How happy you look, Mom,* I said to myself. Then, *Don't you miss us, not even a bit?*

Kristin was watching the screen from behind me. "I guess you can access any of the habitats—or all of them at once, since each has its own monitor," she said. "Is that really your mom?"

I nodded, staring at the screen. I hadn't realized how much I missed her. I was just at the age when I longed for us to talk together woman to woman—not just mother to daughter. But she'd always been so busy. And now . . . I blinked and pulled myself together. "Hey, sorry for hogging this. Want me to access your dome?"

She just shook her head, and I suddenly wondered what had gone wrong in *her* family. She and her brother Bobbie were almost enemies. And now she didn't even want to *look* at her parents.

I turned my attention back to the menus. AUDIO, said one, and I clicked on it. Now I could hear Mom's voice, and she *was* singing, a kind of wordless crooning. It meant she was happy and I was glad of that, even if her happiness came from drugs in her food.

I flipped through the other habitats and caught glimpses of adults eating, reading, playing cards, even sleeping. Snatches of dialogue. I didn't stay to listen—it was too creepy, like spying.

"No children," Kristin said over my shoulder. "I guess they're all here."

But they weren't. When I came to the last habitat—double D—it was night-time. The screen was shadowy and I could only just detect the child lying in bed, dark braids spread across the pillow. I was just about to switch off when the voice began.

"Teresa," it said softly. "Teresa, listen to me. Terebin is calling you. It is time to leave. Get up and get dressed. When you go out, don't forget to put on your protective jumpsuit and your goggles and mask. Don't be afraid, Teresa. Terebin is there, just as you have always dreamed it. Come!"

I cut the audio and swung round to face Kristin. "Wow! So that's how it's done. Jay must have picked Xanadu from my reading aloud and planted it in Gordie's head."

"And he must have created Bobbie's dream of the Big Rock Candy Mountain."

"What else is in here? I wonder . . ." I perused the files. "It would be great if we could find the command to cut off all the force fields—"

"Wouldn't Jay be *furious* if we did that?" Kristin gloated. "I wonder what he'd do to us!"

"If we *could* free them, what could he do about it? All the grown-ups would be against him, once they got here and started eating real food without drugs in it. They'd be back to normal and he wouldn't stand a chance."

Kristin stared. "Drugs?"

"In their food. Didn't you know? You must have noticed how they changed. How they didn't care. I worked out that there was something in the food doing it to them."

Her eyes suddenly filled with tears. "I never guessed. I thought they were just mad at me because . . ." She stopped.

"Go on. Tell me."

She said nothing for a minute, but stood staring at the screen and biting her fingernails. Then it came out in a rush. "It was my fault we were arrested. It was all so stupid. I shot off my big mouth to impress someone. To be noticed. And it got back to WOGPO, the way everything does. I trusted the guy, I really did. He betrayed me, and it was all my fault." She sniffed. "Even here we're not really safe. Jay could be spying on us right now." She looked up at the monitors, at the flickering figures eating, sleeping, watching viddisks—not knowing that all the time they were being watched. "It's so spooky."

"I know, Kristin. I thought we were free here. I was really beginning to believe that this Other Place was a kind of paradise—Gordie's Xanadu—where we were going to get the chance to start over again. But now, when I look at all this . . ." I stared up at the banks of monitors. Spy machines.

"You always were an idealist dreamer, Ally." Kristin's voice was bitter. "I never believed in this freedom story, not for a minute. Which I suppose is why I don't belong, why I can't even try to fit in. I knew we hadn't really escaped WOGPO. No one can. Not ever."

"Not ever?" The voice came from behind us.

My heart almost stopped. Kristin gave a shriek. We both turned to see Jay standing in the doorway. I scrambled to my feet. I used to think that his strange costume of blue and black was like the plumage of some exotic bird. Now it looked truly sinister.

111

CHAPTER SEVEN

Caught red-handed, we stood, guilty and speechless. *There's nowhere to run to, nowhere to hide,* I thought frantically. Jay stood in front of the only exit. Even if we dodged by him, we were likely to lose our way in the labyrinth of passages. He leaned casually against the doorway. He didn't look angry. In fact his mouth was quirked in a smile, though I wasn't sure what that smile meant. His was a hard face to read. Young-old. Severe-friendly. I reached down and tapped the keys that turned off the habitat monitors.

He broke the silence. "You did a good job of tracking me here. My compliments. I had no idea I was being followed."

"Then how did you—?"

"Discover you? Let me give you some advice. Next time you need a torch for some nefarious project, make sure that the wood is not from an incense tree. As soon as I got close to the chute, I smelled it and knew someone had come by. I looked around, and there was the torch itself, hidden behind a boulder. You were ingenious, but not quite clever enough."

As he chatted, I had the feeling that he was just playing with us. *That's just how the World Police behave,* I thought, though I didn't really know if that were so or just hearsay.

"What are you going to do about it?" I blurted out, interrupting him.

"Ah, that's the question, isn't it?" Suddenly alert, he

no longer leaned against the doorway, but strode across the room and faced us. "You had other questions too, didn't you? I heard the last one. *Can anyone ever escape from the World Government Police?* That was it, wasn't it?"

"We already know the answer to that one," Kristin snapped.

"Are you so sure you *do* know the answer?" His voice was lazy, almost teasing, but his eyes narrowed as he looked intently at us.

"Okay, okay." I was sick of games. "I'll ask you. *Can* anyone escape from WOGPO?"

"Maybe."

"*Has* anyone?"

"What do *you* think?"

"What kind of an answer is that?" Kristin shouted.

"No, hold it, Kristin." I hesitated. "I think . . ."

"Go on."

"Well, Kristin and I both came through the force field when we weren't supposed to. That was a kind of escape, wasn't it?"

Jay smiled broadly, but said nothing.

"Oh, you're impossible. I don't know why we went to all this trouble to follow you," Kristin said angrily.

"Trouble? Folly rather! My dear young people, it never occurred to me that you would risk coming down the chute, or I would have put up a barrier."

"Like the one that hides the domes from us?"

"Something like that."

"But why? Why did you call the kids out and not us? Why do you give them tools and look after them, and yet let them think they're independent? You've been good to them, I can see that. But then there's all this . . ." I waved my hand at the array of monitors and speakers. "All this secrecy. Eavesdropping on the habitats. So either you're a member of the police force or a WOG spy. How can you be bad and good at the same time? You don't make sense. Which are you?"

"Perhaps a bit of both. Humans are usually not all one thing or the other, are they?" He was interrupted by a chime. He exclaimed and brushed by me to seat himself at the keyboard. He accessed the last dome—DD—and in the dim light we could see the young girl wrestling with the outside door, which was almost too big for her to open. A soft haunting voice urged her on. "You can do it, Teresa. You can reach Terebin. Terebin is calling you. Come . . ."

Jay cut the sound quickly. "I must be there to welcome her when she arrives. I was on my way when your incense torch led me astray. A false scent, you might say. You must wait here until I get back. That is an order, Ally, Kristin. Don't attempt to leave. The labyrinth is a subtle puzzle and your chances of escaping without guidance are almost nil."

He turned in a swirl of blue and black ribbons and was gone.

"Well, what do you make of *that*, Kristin?" I said into the silence.

"He didn't say he *wasn't* the police, did he?"

"On the other hand, he didn't say he was. The problem is, he didn't really say anything. Hold on, did you notice that it was night-time in that dome but broad daylight in mine?"

"So?"

"I don't know. It's just one more weird thing, isn't it? It's as if time inside the domes is being manipulated. Or they're all on different times—like time zones on Earth."

"So? Different time zones. What does that have to do with who Jay is or what's really going on?" Kristin's voice was edgy.

"It might be important. What I mean is, in our dome there were dozens of boxes of jigsaw puzzles, but not one of them had a picture on the top. You just had to take it on faith that all the pieces did belong to the puzzle inside, and start off making the straight edges as a frame and then work inwards to find out what kind of picture it was. I think we've got to use the same technique here. We've got a lot of puzzle pieces and individually they don't make any sense. But the more pieces we collect, the more likely we are to find out what the picture's about, and maybe even put it together."

"Okay. So how are we going to find extra pieces?"

"Poke around this computer system for a start. There's bound to be a lot more in these files than access to the domes."

I sat down at the central console and began to play with the keyboard. I pulled down a menu, scanned it and tried another.

"Ha, I've found something!" I clicked onto the familiar logo of WOG. Another menu. Personnel. Policies. Security Council . . . "Security Council! Hey, that sounds interesting." I clicked again.

RESTRICTED INFORMATION. PASSWORD PLEASE.

"Too bad we don't know Jay's password." Kristin leaned over my shoulder. "Try JAY."

"Too short and too obvious."

"Try it anyway. What have you got to lose?"

115

I typed in JAY.

ACCESS DENIED.

"I told you so. Any other ideas?"

"Doesn't he remind you of that bird? Those blue-black ribbons fluttering around like feathers."

"And the way his hair grows to a peak on top," I added excitedly. "Like a blue jay's. That's more like it."

I keyed in BLUEJAY and waited for the magic open sesame.

ACCESS DENIED. FAILURE TO INPUT THE CORRECT PASSWORD AT THE NEXT ATTEMPT WILL RESULT IN THE CLOSURE OF ALL SECURE SYSTEMS.

I groaned. "And we totally wasted our first try. We haven't a hope of getting it right. Not in only one more guess."

"Too much to expect that it would be so easy," Kristin said glumly. "He wouldn't have left us here alone with this system unless he was sure we wouldn't be able to access it. He's a tricky devil, that Jay. I know I'm right not to trust him."

I found myself defending him. "You must admit he's worked hard to protect the kids and give them a chance to develop in this new world."

"That's all very well, Ally. But why didn't he just leave them in their domes in the first place? He called them out. We heard that audio, didn't we? Calling Teresa out? Basically he's kidnapped them, so once he's taken them away from their parents, he's responsible for them. No great virtue on his part."

Kristin was right. But she was also wrong. Everything about Jay seemed to be both black and white. He was good. He was bad. He was a spy. He was a friend.

Kidnapper. Rescuer. "Tricky's the word," I muttered, my fingers lying loosely on the keys.

Then my brain suddenly made the connection. Tricky. *Trickster.* Our class had studied tricksters in a course on the mythology of ancient cultures. I had found it quite interesting, once I'd screened out the obvious propaganda bits designed to show us kids what a far better, more advanced and kindly culture our World Government was providing than anything that had gone before.

In the beginning days, I remembered, when people believed in magic and a variety of gods, tricksters were important. They were ambiguous, two-faced—tricky, in fact. They had all sorts of power, but they weren't grand and aloof; they played jokes on humans and weren't always to be trusted. They had to be treated cautiously, because they were also the givers of gifts, the bringers of fire, the teachers of important life-giving facts. They were represented in many ways in different lands, but always in the guise of an animal. A trickster might be a raven or a coyote, a rabbit or, perhaps, a blue jay.

"Got it!" I said aloud and confidently keyed in TRICKSTER.

ACCESS GRANTED, said the monitor. We were in!

Now all we had to do was to ask the right questions and with luck we would get the answers we wanted. Time flew by as we read the whole hidden history of the World Government's plans for expansion and the role that WOGPO was playing in furthering those aims.

Each piece of information led us to another, and we found ourselves getting deeper and deeper into the affairs of the World Government. It was like exploring a house where each room led to another and another,

117

each more elaborately furnished than the one before.
And our search was every bit as fascinating.

We came at last to the secret minutes of a meeting.
"Wow!" we whispered in chorus as it scrolled across the
screen in front of us.

MINUTES OF SPECIAL MEETING OF SECU-
RITY COUNCIL OF THE WORLD GOVERN-
MENT, GENEVA, MAY 18, 2154, CONCERNING
PROJECT BOTANY BAY.

Attending: President Gloria Miguel
          Vice-president Pierre Fontaine
          Chief of World Police Gordon Black
          Chief advisor World Bank Frieda Hoffmann
          Coordinator International Aid and
            Cooperation Soo Lee

Also present, as special witness, Chief Scientist for
Project Botany Bay, Dr. Julius Kereluk.

MIGUEL: This meeting has been called to acquaint you
with the findings of Project Botany Bay. I take this
opportunity to welcome Dr. Julius Kereluk to Geneva
and to thank him for his presence.

LEE: Madame President, I am puzzled by the fact that
no position papers have been circulated regarding this
project. How are we expected to make judgements
based on no prior knowledge?

BLACK: I agree, Madame President. This is most unusual.

MIGUEL: Ladies and gentlemen, please bear with me
for a short while. Once you have heard of Dr. Kereluk's
startling innovation, you will understand the need for
complete secrecy.

BLACK: Is this meeting being recorded?

MIGUEL: Yes, but only on my secure interior system,
for replay at future meetings of this council.

BLACK: Very well. My apologies for interrupting.

MIGUEL: Perhaps you will begin, Dr. Kereluk.

KERELUK: With your permission I will explain the Botany Bay project as a narrative. When I have finished my story, I believe all will be clear. The project began with the discovery, a number of years ago, of an effective short-range matter transmitter. Major Black will be familiar with one aspect of its use, since it was released to the World Government Police for the effective instantaneous deployment of force in situations such as public uprisings following floods, famine or other natural disasters. In this context the transmitter—SMT—was very effective. However, when overcrowding in some parts of the world became severe and caused civilian riots and unrest, even the instant presence of the police on the scene was not sufficient to defuse the situation. My scientists began working on a new and imaginative application of SMT technology, that is, the seeding of liveable planets with groups from Earth—

LEE (interrupting): But we are all aware of this. The attempt to colonize has been a total failure.

KERELUK: Ms. Lee is correct. We found that even when seeding large family groups, the shock of transference to a totally alien environment, from which there could be no return, destabilized the settlers. Without exception the groups—which were, of course, being monitored—broke apart, reverted to primitive behaviour patterns and eventually died out. Admittedly it was a disaster. Moreover it was becoming increasingly difficult to recruit volunteers without compromising the necessary secrecy of the whole enterprise. It was at this point that Project Botany Bay was first suggested.

FONTAINE: Why Botany Bay?

KERELUK: It was named for a historic penal colony that was established on the then-unexplored continent of Australia by the British government at the end of the eighteenth century. A masterly solution to the problem of overcrowded jails. Of course you can see the potential. We could continue our experiments in seeding unexplored planets with no risk to security, and at the same time empty our overcrowded prisons, thus lessening the tax burden on law-abiding citizens.

BLACK: But seeding a planet with thieves and murderers seems an even more risky venture than your previous attempt.

KERELUK: Indeed! But it occurred to a bright criminologist on my staff that the Botany Bay project might provide an excellent way of ridding our society of dissidents. Not only are they a burden to the taxpayer, but their ideas have also been thought to contaminate entire prison populations.

BLACK: Dr. Kereluk is quite correct. The riots at Detention Centre Thirty-two last year were the result of infiltration by only two dissidents. *Two*, mark you! In the old days such people undermining our society would have been quietly eliminated. Mass executions and burials. Removal by helicopter and disposal over the ocean. And so on.

LEE: Quite. But such solutions are barbaric and cannot be considered in a civilized society such as ours. Even the memory of such incidents is distasteful.

KERELUK: Precisely. How much more humane if the disappearance of dissidents were complete—if they quit Earth, with which they seemed dissatisfied, to start again on another planet?

HOFFMANN: An elegant solution, Dr. Kereluk. When do you intend to start this experiment?

KERELUK: It has already begun.

(Clamour of voices, unidentifiable.)

KERELUK: Please, ladies and gentlemen. I did consult Madame Miguel. Members of my staff have made discreet inquiries in each of your departments and applied the findings to a computer model, with various options. In every case Project Botany Bay was the preferred solution.

FONTAINE: How long has this covert operation been going on?

KERELUK: The first attempt, involving a group of some fifty dissidents, was made five years ago. Unfortunately it failed, in exactly the same way as the colony seeded with volunteers. I was about to abandon the experiment when a psychologist on my staff suggested that a colony of children might stand a better chance of success.

LEE: Children? That is absurd.

KERELUK: My first reaction also. But then the value of children as colonists was pointed out to me. They are imaginative and open-minded. They are not burdened by habits and memories that would be useless—and perhaps psychologically as well as physically danger-ous—in an alien world. Those of you who are familiar with Earth history will recall that many early colonists met with disaster, starving in the midst of plenty, for instance, as they persisted in habits of clothing, food and social structure that were actually hazardous in their new environment.

LEE: True. And if I recall correctly, in many cases these innocents abroad were saved from total disaster by the native inhabitants of the lands they were occupying.

But of course such aid would not be available on an uninhabited planet.

KERELUK: Ms. Lee is correct. That was the first problem. The second was how to arrange for the secret removal of a carefully chosen group of children, ones who were well educated, healthy, balanced. The answer turned out to be extremely simple and elegant—to arrest not only troublesome dissidents, but their children also. This has been done, and thirty family groups have been sent to a suitable planet, within reach of communications satellites, which we have named Botany Bay.

HOFFMANN: I applaud the elegance of Dr. Kereluk's solution to the problem of dissidence and, in the long run, that of overcrowding, since I presume that once these groups have stabilized, members of the general population will also be sent. But how did your solution differ from the other attempts to seed planets, attempts that failed so miserably?

KERELUK: The difference lay in the radical solution proposed by the young psychologist I mentioned earlier. He recommended that we realize the full potential of the children by forcibly removing them from their family units and giving them a new kind of identity, no longer as part of a nuclear family of father, mother and child, but of a larger cooperative grouping.

LEE: Surely not on their own?

KERELUK: Partially. They are under discreet observation. Once they form a cohesive unit, the parents will be released into the new groups where, hopefully, they will learn the new social structures and adapt to them. The adults are being made amenable to their new role through the use of psychotropic drugs.

FONTAINE: Theoretically a brilliant solution to outstanding problems on Earth. I presume that once a stable society has been established, World Government will be able to claim the planet and develop its natural resources?

KERELUK: That would seem to be a natural end result.

FONTAINE: You sound doubtful.

KERELUK: Not at all. There must be an eventual payback of the vast start-up costs of this project. I would hope though that this will not occur too soon. This new society will need time to stabilize first.

LEE: Madame President, before you ask for our approval of the continuation of Project Botany Bay, I think it would be appropriate for us to have the opportunity of cross-examining this psychologist.

MIGUEL: A reasonable suggestion. Dr. Kereluk, will you arrange for this individual to appear before our council within the next week?

(Pause)

MIGUEL: Dr. Kereluk?

KERELUK: I'm afraid that will not be possible, Madame President. The man in question is not available.

MIGUEL: Make it so, if you please!

KERELUK: I mean he really is not available. He volunteered to go to Botany Bay to oversee his project . . .

As I was reading these last words off the screen, before I had entirely taken in the implications of Project Botany Bay, Kristin gripped my shoulder. "He's coming back," she hissed.

Quickly I exited the program and switched back to "Habitats". By the time Jay entered the room we were

123

both looking innocently at Habitat W, watching my mother paint her wild mural.

"Sorry to keep you waiting so long," he apologized.

I was about to say that the time had flown when Kristin got in ahead of me. "Thought you'd never get back." She scowled. "We were of two minds whether to risk finding our own way out of here."

"That would have been unwise, as I told you. Well now." He leaned against one of the consoles and stared at us, his face grave. "What *am* I going to do with the pair of you?"

CHAPTER EIGHT

"Well, you can't leave us down here," Kristin bluffed. Though she was often gritty and downright rude, I had to admire her courage and quickness now. I was speechless—the revelation of the secret council meeting was still making my head spin.

Jay gave a slow smile, but I saw a frown line between his eyes. "I could if I chose," he retorted. "You might find the sleeping quarters a bit rough—I have no intention of giving mine up to you—but I have plenty of supplies, a matter transmitter and access to anything else I might need. So your presence down here would not be a particular burden on me."

"You . . . you don't really intend to keep us here, do you?" I stammered.

"I might have to. You must realize, since you are both intelligent young women, that if I let you go, I will have to trust you not to reveal my secret to the young ones."

Secret? But he doesn't know we've seen inside his secret files.

"I don't understand," I said hesitantly.

"Oh, you know, Ally," Kristin broke in. "All this fancy computer stuff. Like a secret command centre. Like WOGPO in fact. No wonder you don't want us to tell the kids. They think you're magical. A wonderful kind of Pied Piper. Aha! That's it, isn't it, Jay? You're a member of WOGPO, spying on us all."

Jay actually flushed and stood upright, no longer leaning casually against the console. "I assure you I am not."

125

"Why should we believe what you say?" I tried to follow Kristin's blustering lead. "Not after this huge lie." I waved my arm at the installation around us.

He sighed. "You have no idea how difficult you two are making this decision for me."

"It might make things easier if you told us the truth," I suggested.

"Starting with who you really are and why you're here," Kristin added.

Jay began to pace up and down the room. "If I tell you what it's all about, will you swear to keep the knowledge from the children? It's important. The whole experiment depends on their belief in their independence—"

"Which is a lie," Kristin interrupted. "Because we know you're in charge."

"Not entirely. Little by little they're learning to make their own decisions."

"You've given them Earth clothing, Earth artifacts," she persisted.

"Of course. That's legitimate for a beginning colony. In the olden days the settlers from the *Mayflower* didn't land in North America empty-handed. They brought agricultural implements, pots and pans, whatever they thought they would need from the old country. Then, as the years went by, they gradually became more self-sufficient."

"So eventually you intend to stop supplying us with clothes, and we'll have to weave our own? What from? How will we learn? You've been providing us with meat, so we can't even make clothes out of skins the way people once did, even if we knew how," I added.

Jay stopped pacing and spread out his arms. "You see how much I need you two on my side! You're invaluable to the youngsters with your adult knowledge and youthful freedom to improvise. Clothes out of skins!"

"Oh, don't patronize us, Jay!" Kristin snapped and he laughed mockingly.

"You don't really mean to leave us underground, do you?" I challenged him. Again he laughed. This time his face did not contradict itself, and I saw the laughter spread to his eyes.

"I suppose I can't. But it is vital that you keep the secret of my hidey-hole, at the very least because of the danger of the chute. Will you promise?"

We looked at each other and nodded. "That makes sense."

"Only . . ." I hesitated.

"Yes?"

"You said you needed the two of us, as if we were part of your plan to—to help the children grow. So how come you let Kristin be thrown out of the community? That was unbelievably cruel."

"It was the choice of the young people," he said quickly, but his cheeks flushed. "It was curious how they turned against her, especially since you, Alison, seem to have no problem integrating with the youngsters."

"You're talking as if Kristin were an animal in an experiment, not a human being. You should have helped her. At the very least you could have given her a knife and a tinderbox."

"Not interfering was a hard decision," Jay admitted. "I had just given the children the power to make their own decisions by consensus. If I had immediately taken it away again . . ." He shrugged. "If it had been winter I would have intervened. But Kristin has been in no danger."

"Just going out of my mind with loneliness, that's all."
Kristin spat out the words. "I don't know who I hate the
most—you or the kids."

"Hate me if it makes you feel better, but not the kids.
They're young. They make mistakes. But what they're
doing, learning to work together and achieve consensus—that's an invaluable experience."

"And I was just a guinea pig for their experiments?"

"I suppose so. I'm not proud of the choice I had to
make."

"We're going to change all that, Kristin," I said firmly.
"I'll persuade them to take you back. No more nights
alone in the forest for you."

"Thanks a lot, Ally. But I don't want any favours."

"No favours. I need a friend too, Kristin. I've been
lonely having no one to share what I know—what I can't
tell them."

"Not even Gordie? I thought you two were friends."

"Tell him we're on an alien planet? That we're never
going to go home? He's only eight, Kristin. How could
I?"

"That's settled then," Jay said firmly. "I'll take you
back now. Don't ever risk coming down the chute by
yourselves again. You were darn lucky that you didn't
drown or wander through the underground passages
forever."

I felt sure he was exaggerating. Finding his secret lair
had not been so difficult after all.

Jay must have seen the disbelief on my face. "Why
don't you lead us out of here, Alison?" he said craftily.

I looked uncertainly at Kristin. "Come on," she said,
"we'll both lead the way." We set out briskly. The
passage that we had seen Jay emerge from when we

were hiding was on our left, I remembered, so I confidently turned right at the first intersection on the way back. It seemed a shorter distance than on the way in, but returning always does seem to take less time than exploring new territory, I told myself.

Kristin didn't hesitate either. The passage began to slope downwards. Had we climbed on the way to Jay's secret room? I couldn't remember. Then I noticed that the walls were rough and beaded with moisture, not smoothly finished with a laser beam, as the main passage was.

I stopped and laughed. "How silly. I guess we turned too soon."

"Yes. It must be the *second* turn on the right," Kristin added.

Jay said nothing, but politely stood aside for us to pass so that we were again in the lead.

"The main passage has been lasered smooth," I remarked. "That should make it easy to identify."

"Ye-es." Kristin paused before we entered the main passage and ran her finger over the rock wall. "But the beginning of this side passage was smoothed down too. It was only later on that . . ." Her voice trailed off.

"Oh, come on. I'm sure we've got it right now," I said briskly. "Here's the correct turn."

We walked on. I was beginning to realize that it had been a long time since we'd eaten our scanty meal of flatbread at the top of the chute. I wondered how many hours we'd spent underground. Would supper be over by the time we got back? Roast meat, I remembered, as my stomach clenched with emptiness and my mouth suddenly filled with saliva.

I swallowed and tried to pay attention to the way we

were going. Another fork in the passage. We had deliberately alternated right and left turns on our way in, but which had been our final choice in the moment before we heard Jay coming? Left or right? He was humming now as he had been then. A very irritating tuneless hum.

"Left?" I looked at Kristin.

"I thought right," she said uncertainly. "But maybe I was wrong."

I sighed. "Okay, Jay. You've made your point. Will you please get us out of here?"

"It'll be my pleasure."

With Jay in the lead it seemed no time at all before the noise told us that we were approaching the chute. He ignored the torch we had left behind a rock and from an inside pocket produced a small flashlight with an intense beam that brilliantly lit the steps up to the surface. If we had seen as clearly on our way down the crooked, spray-slicked steps, I doubt if we would have risked it. Even with Jay holding the light, and with the rope to hang on to, climbing out was an ordeal I never wanted to repeat.

Safely at the top and far enough from the thunder of the falling water for us to hear ourselves think, Jay stopped. "If you follow the trail, it'll bring you safely back to the village. But you'll have to hurry. It'll be dark before long."

"You're not coming with us?"

He shook his head. "You'll be fine on your own."

As he turned away, I called out, "Jay. Wait a minute!"

"Yes?"

"Isn't there a way we can get in touch with you—in case we need anything?"

"You know I come to the village every five days or so."

"I mean alone, where we can talk. We still have so many questions."

He shook his head. "You don't really need me that much. As for your questions . . ." He smiled. "In due course. Now, off with you. Hurry." He waved his hand and vanished once more into the darkness of the cave and the thunder of the chute.

It wasn't until we were almost at the village, having hurried along the easy trail that Jay had used rather than the ridge from which we had tracked him, that I suddenly stopped.

Kristin bumped into me. "What's up, Ally?"

"Jay never did tell us who he really is."

"Just that he's not WOGPO—if we can believe him. Tricky Jay. But I think I know," she said.

"Go on."

"Remember the psychologist who thought up this whole Botany Bay project. Doctor What's-his-name—Kereluk—said that he'd volunteered to oversee it in person."

"Jay?"

"Think about it. Isn't it the perfect explanation of what he's doing here?"

"I guess so."

We walked on in silence. I could see the light of the fire glimmering between the trees. In the gathering dusk it drew us into its welcoming glow. Supper would soon be over and the children in bed. But before they went, I had a score to settle.

Kristin and I ate in haste, for the meal was almost over

when we arrived. I chose to sit at the far end of the table and made room for Kristin next to me.

Gordie scrambled from his place. "She's not supposed to be here, Ally," he whispered in my ear. "She doesn't belong."

"Who says?"

"Everyone." He was biting his lip, which he only did when he was really upset.

"After dinner I'll talk to everyone. I'll ask permission. It's going to be all right," I added firmly. Gordie hesitated, then went back to his friends.

The other children stared and whispered, but said nothing to us. Perhaps they were surprised at the change in Kristin's appearance. With her hair freshly washed and with clean clothes, she looked very different from the outcast who snatched food from the table and ate standing, ready to run.

As soon as we had eaten, I stood up. "I have a request to make of the community. Will you hear me?"

The children looked at each other, nodded, and then Tomas stood up. "We'll hear you, Ally."

I took a deep breath, determined to get it right. "Before I got here, Kristin arrived among you, and she was older than any of you. She did not understand your ways. She was not helped to understand, and you rejected her. If I had been a member of the community then, I would have begged you to change your mind, because I know she has so much to offer. Now that I *am* here, part of the community, I ask you to reconsider your decision and accept Kristin."

I sat down. Tomas looked at Bryan and he nodded. "We need to have a meeting, but it's getting dark. Shall we meet tomorrow after breakfast?"

There was a general assent, followed by a hasty clearing of the table. "I've been away all day," I said. "Perhaps it would be fair for me to do the dishes. Kristin can help."

This was solemnly approved, and Kristin and I scraped off the wooden platters and scrubbed them clean while the younger ones made ready for bed.

"So far, so good," I said quietly. "But you *must* try not to get their backs up. Look at it from their point of view. They've suddenly got the freedom to design a new world, and are really getting into the swing of it, when a couple of almost-adults arrive. You can see how they must be afraid that we'll try to take over."

"Okay, okay. I'll behave, though I've got to tell you that your meekness really sets my teeth on edge."

"It's not meekness, honestly. I'm trying to walk in their shoes. There, that's the lot. Time for bed."

"But I'm not 'in' yet. How can I sleep here?" Kristin's expression changed, and I realized that under the bluff of her bullying attitude she was very insecure.

"It'll be okay. I'll ask Kate if you can share my bed for tonight. We'll manage, head to toe—but if you kick me, I'll push you out."

There was neither kicking nor pushing. We were both so tired that neither of us moved until morning. I joined the rest of the community for the formal meeting after breakfast, and there, with the talking stick in my hand, I argued Kristin's case. It was not as difficult as I was afraid it might be. In fact it was mostly a question of flattering Bobbie, who was now independent enough in his own right that he wasn't much bothered by the possibility of his big sister bossing him around.

"But what can she *do*?" someone asked.

"Everything you can. Find roots and berries and fruit—she got good at that when she was on her own. She'll help dig latrines and build new huts. She's got much better muscles than I have."

My feeble joke got a laugh, but the discussion wasn't quite over yet. "You're good at botany and stuff. You helped make bread and discover new herbs," Claire said.

"I know Kristin will be just as useful. But anyway, are you being quite fair? Think about it. You accepted each other when you came through from the habitats without worrying what each of you could do. Why be so tough on Kristin?"

They talked about this and did some arguing, but never interrupting, always passing the talking stick gravely from one to another. I found myself thinking how fascinated Jay, as a psychologist, would be with their discussions. The youngsters *were* finding their own way of making a new kind of society, one in which the value of everyone's opinion was important. When they voted—and it was unanimous, with even Bobbie saying okay—I knew that what Jay was trying to do was working.

The days went by. No new children came through from the habitats. Teresa had been the last, and now we numbered thirty-four. It became cooler and the days shortened. Our storehouse of nuts and dried fruit was almost full. Someone suggested that we ought to have a communal hall, a place where we could eat together when it was too cold or rainy to eat at the big table outside, and where we could gather and talk in the evenings when winter was really upon us.

We had many discussions about how to build a house that was so much larger than our simple sleeping huts. How would we support the roof? I knew it could be done. The aboriginal longhouses in both central and western Canada and in New Zealand proved it was possible. Where there was wood, there was a way of building. I only wished I had paid more attention in history class—but how could I have guessed that one day I might be called upon to help design such a place?

Kristin and I were the only near adults. Bryan and Tomas were strong, well-muscled boys, but they were not fully grown. Could we really cut down big trees and raise beams to support a roof without injuring anyone? The walls of our huts were only saplings, piled loosely between end-posts and caulked with mud. The structure of a longhouse would be very different.

We held a lot of meetings, drawing plans on the underside of tree bark with charcoal plucked from the remains of the fire. In the end we settled for the simplest possible structure, an outer frame of posts planted firmly in the ground at our chosen spot. We gave the roof a pitch by designing the posts about a metre and a half longer at the back than the front.

It was going to be a huge job. Could we do it? In order to build a house big enough to hold the whole community, we needed an area of about twenty-seven square metres. As we made our plans, I was thankful that I'd always been good at math.

The roof was the biggest problem. We discussed it for ages, and then decided that if we could find a slender tree long enough to span the house from back to front, we would be able to lay saplings close together from side wall to centre and from the centre to the other side wall. We could then tie the saplings down with creepers, since we had no nails.

"But that's not enough to keep out the rain," Kate said at this point. "What'll we cover the saplings with? We'll have to use something light."

"Grass is light," Anna said.

"It'd blow away," Lois said, and she and Claire began to giggle.

"Not if we tied it in bundles and laid the bundles from the bottom upwards, tied to the branches underneath," Alicia said excitedly. And so it was decided.

We didn't have the right tools to make planks for the side walls, but the bark from some really large trees might work. We would have to try. As we talked, the longhouse became a realistic possibility. But what a monumental amount of work it was going to be! What could be done in a few days with a power saw and a bunch of nails was going to take us weeks—if indeed we were successful. We had knives in the community, but only one axe.

"Perhaps it would make more sense if we asked Jay for a prefab plasteel dome and avoided all this grief," Kristin muttered to me when we were on supper duty one evening.

I thought about it and shook my head. "We've got to learn to be self-sufficient, to use what we've got."

"And what happens when the axe wears out and the knives rust away?"

"Give me a break, Kristin!"

"I'm only being logical, Ally. Sooner or later it's going to happen, and what will we do then?"

"Go back to the beginnings of technology, I suppose. Stone axes. Flint or obsidian knives. Okay?"

She nodded and flashed a grin at me. "Just testing whether you could unthink the 'normal' way of doing things."

I glanced over my shoulder to make sure we weren't being overheard. "You know, I think Jay's on to something. The youngest ones have the best chance of adapting. Like Alicia's idea of using bundled grass for the roof. Oh, I know thatches were used for roofing in the olden days, but *she* didn't know that. She invented it for our present need in *this* place. And I bet they'll come up with even more and better ideas as we need them."

"You still think Jay is a good guy, don't you?" Kristin teased. "Ally, you're so naive!"

Villain? Hero? I wasn't sure; however I went to bed that night feeling pretty secure about the future of our unnamed planet. *But we're going to have to think of a proper name for it,* I thought sleepily. *Not Xanadu, nor Big Rock Candy Mountain. Something that's special to this place.* And I chuckled to myself as I imagined the huge discussions there would be about the possible name, and I wondered whether, with thirty-four different ideas, we would ever reach consensus. Then I fell asleep.

Next day we began work on the longhouse. A knotted vine became the measure for the distance between post holes, and I marked a long straight stick to indicate how deep the holes should be. It probably wasn't exactly one metre—I had guessed the distance from the tips of the fingers of one outstretched hand to the opposite shoulder joint—but that didn't matter. So long as we stuck to the same measurement throughout, we wouldn't get into trouble. I remembered reading on a history disk, back in the school library on faraway Earth, that once upon a time the standard measurement was the length of the king's foot, and other measures were the length of a thumb and of a forearm. So now we were starting our own tradition.

None of us had ever cut down a tree before—why, most of us had never *seen* a tree except in a botanical garden. I had thought this task would be simple, but when I tried it the axe bounced back dangerously, threatening my legs and anyone else close by. After that we practised until we learned to hit at exactly the right angle. The actual felling of the first tree, which took much longer than I thought, was a disaster. The trunk split with a fearsome crack and crashed to the ground, narrowly missing Kristin.

"Hey, watch it!"

"I'm sorry, I'm sorry. It just *went!*"

We looked at the ragged and ruined stump. "Maybe if we notch into one side of the tree and then cut from the other it'll work better," Kate suggested. And it did.

Over the next two weeks, working in short shifts, Kristin, Tomas, Brian, Kate and I managed to chop down the fourteen trees we needed for the frame and the one for the central roof support. Meanwhile the younger ones, well away from the danger of falling trees, were busy digging post holes at the site. They did a perfect job: the holes fell in straight lines, and the corners made a good ninety degree angle.

"However did you get the sides so straight?" I asked. After all, they had only a knotted vine as a measure, and vines tend to bend.

"We just stuck twigs in the ground and squinted along them till we got a straight line," Gordie told me proudly.

It was Gordie, too, who came up with the answer to

one of our most perplexing problems. The large pieces of bark that we wanted to use for walls just wouldn't lie flat. When we were heating water to wash the dishes after one of Jay's roast meat meals, Gordie noticed that the pole holding the pot over the fire began to bend.

"Why does it do that?" he asked.

"The steam must make it soft," Merry suggested.

"So we could steam the bark, couldn't we?" Gordie said excitedly. And that's what we did. We held the sheets above the pot until they softened, and then we piled them on the flat ground with stones on top. It worked perfectly. We also found that when the bark was moist and pliable, we could easily make holes in it. Later we threaded twine through these holes to fasten the bark to the upright posts.

The twine itself was prepared by the very youngest ones in the community, sitting under a shade tree, scraping at vines with sharp-edged stones until the bark was gone and a pliable tough twine remained. "And we can go on scraping till it's as fine as string," Teresa said excitedly. "Why, we can make nets and . . . and all sorts of stuff."

Little by little we were discovering the possibilities of our new world.

CHAPTER NINE

Just as the leaves began to yellow and a fine frost crisped the grass of the glade, the longhouse was finished, and we began to plan a special celebration for the next time Jay brought meat. Meantime we erected a shelter over the big fireplace, leaving the sides open to let out the smoke. We still needed to cook outdoors, because we had not yet found a safe way to install a fireplace in our new longhouse without the risk of burning it down.

We planned and waited. The next five-day went by, and Jay did not come. We weren't actually hungry. We ground seeds and baked flatbread every other day, and we had our winter store of nuts and dried fruit; but meat gave us more energy, and we were afraid to dig too deeply into our winter supplies until we knew how long and how severe the winter might be. "Where's Jay?" the small ones asked. "Why hasn't he come?"

Kristin and I wondered guiltily if his absence had anything to do with our discovery of his underground hideaway. Meanwhile we had to find other protein foods. Using the finest twine that the youngsters made, we knotted nets and caught plump and tasty fish in the bigger streams, which we baked on stones by the fire. We also learned to catch some of the small animals that scurried through the undergrowth around our glade, using traps made of cord and bent sapling wood. All of us began to look more closely for signs of where these creatures ran, and again the small children were best at this, their sharp eyes discovering tiny runways among the grass and brush.

Our first experience of skinning and gutting these small animals was a dismal failure, and we had to throw the mangled remains on the fire. But with practice we became quite skilful. The problem was that it took at least six of these small creatures—we called them "greenies", because of the colour of their fur—to make a meal for thirty-four hungry people.

We discovered that they tasted better and went further when we simmered them in the pot with root vegetables and herbs until the meat fell off the bones and we were left with a nourishing and tasty broth. But this method took a lot of time, and we longed for the rich flavour and the fattiness of the beasts Jay brought us. Fat was really lacking in our diet, and as it grew colder, we realized we would need even more of it.

One morning about ten days after that first frost, we found on the table a bow and about a dozen arrows. They had been used. The flight feathers of two had been broken and repaired, so we knew they had to be Jay's. The message was clear: you're on your own, kids!

Bryan, Tomas, Kristin, Kate and I began to learn to use them, going to another glade where there was no danger of a child's running between us and an errant arrow. We marked a blaze on a tree at the height, we guessed, of a large animal's heart. Then we took it in turns to draw the bow and let the arrows fly. And fly they did! In all directions.

It took another five days—and many sore wrists and arms—before we learned how taut to draw the bowstring for the arrow to fly a certain distance and hit the mark, how to hold one's face alongside the drawn bow and sight along the arrow, and how—most difficult of all—to be very still and steady in that second when the arrow was released.

In the end we found that Bryan and I were the best shots, with Tomas and Kristin close behind. Kate just didn't have the eye for it and had to give up. We decided that we would pair up to hunt, Tomas and Bryan alternating with Kristin and me. We made a holder for the arrows out of a curl of bark stitched along the bottom and up the side, with a braided vine sling so it could be carried over the shoulder.

Already we were beginning to search out the small natural paths that bigger animals forced through thickets and between trees. We began to develop a new kind of awareness of small signs we had never noticed before—the shadowy print of a hoof in a patch of frost before the sun melted it, a neat pile of droppings, a tangle of coarse hair caught in a bush. We knew that big animals passed by. It was just that we never saw them.

Obviously they drank at streams and grazed for their fodder. All we had to do was find the places they frequented—and the right time of day. Since we never saw them, we guessed that they were only active in the very early morning or the late evening. During the day, when we were around, they probably rested, hidden in the forest.

Once our plans were made, Kristin and I took a day's supply of food and left the village long before the sun was up, aiming for the place where a small river widened into a sheltered bay. In the mud at the water's edge we had found, during previous visits, a number of fresh hoof prints, so we guessed this had to be a favourite drinking place.

We found a comfortable spot where a fallen log made a seat and where we were screened by bushes but still had a clear view, framed by trees, of the little beach. We drew for the privilege of the first shot and I won, though I was not sure if winning was what I wanted. *When the moment actually comes, will I be able to kill a big animal?* I asked myself anxiously. I wasn't sure I could. We sat patiently, still and silent. I had the bow in my hand, the arrows at my side.

At last the sun rose, a golden ball over the hill behind us, and slanted through the trees, marking the beach with stripes of light and shadow. We never saw them come. It was like magic. One moment we saw only the river dancing in the sun. The next moment two animals stood by the water's edge, their coats striped with the same light and shade as the sand. The head of one bent towards the water. The other remained alert, its head erect, nose twitching, its single horn pointing to the sky. It was standing sideways to me—the best possible shot.

Slowly I reached for an arrow, notched it against the bowstring and slowly drew the bowstring back to its fullest tension. I sighted along the dark wood, aiming for the place just below and behind the shoulder where I guessed the animal's heart would be. I took a deep breath and released the arrow.

In the very second of the arrow's flight the animal tensed and moved. The other stopped drinking and raised its head and at once they were off, bounding through the water, kicking up the spray in a sparkle of diamonds.

"Bad luck," said Kristin.

"I was *sure* I'd got it." I couldn't believe I was mistaken, and when I went down to the little beach to retrieve my arrow, I knew I had not been. "The arrow's gone. And look, there's blood. Oh, how awful!"

The few drops of bright red accused me from a patch of gravel. "We can't leave it, not when it's wounded."

"Of course not, Ally. But it wasn't your fault. It moved."

The idea of the beast hurting, maybe slowly bleeding to death, was too horrible to think about. I tried to push the picture—and the guilt—out of my mind and concentrate on tracking the wounded beast.

It wasn't difficult. A steady trickle of blood left spots on the ground, on fallen leaves. The animal was not taking a straight path, but zigzagging to and fro, now following an existing trail, now leaping a low bush and heading off at an angle.

At one point we came upon a bigger pool of blood and the shaft of the arrow, its point missing. Obviously it had caught in the tangle of underbrush and been broken off, leaving the point still in the animal's side. I bit my lip till it hurt, blinking back tears, imagining the beast's pain.

We stopped briefly to drink from one of the many streams that criss-crossed our path and we ate a piece of flatbread each but then plodded on grimly, never noticing that the trail was leading us farther and farther away from the village.

In the end we almost tripped over our poor quarry. It had weakened and finally fallen. It lay on its side, its neck extended, its eyes rolled back so the whites were visible. I could see the dark stain matting the fur of its side. I knelt beside it and laid my hand on its neck. "I'm so sorry," I whispered.

Kristin took the knife from her waistband, and I shut my eyes.

"It's over," she said gently and I turned away and finally burst into tears.

By the time I'd pulled myself together, Kristin had efficiently gutted the beast and buried the remains. She washed her hands and the knife in a nearby stream and used the knife to cut a sturdy sapling.

"You've got string in that bag of yours?" she asked.

"Sure. What for?" I rubbed my hand over my wet face and dug in my bag for a ball of vine-cord.

"It'll be a lot easier to carry than drag." She tied the animal's feet together fore and aft, and slipped the pole between them. "Come on. We'd better get started. It'll be dark before we know it."

It was only then that I realized the day was slipping away fast. The sky was now a clear blue-green and the sun was dipping below the trees. I took the front pole—feeling that I couldn't bear to look at the results of our butchery—and we set out retracing our steps, spot by spot. There was the place where we had found the broken arrow. And there the place where the animal had crashed through a patch of bushes.

And then we lost it. In daylight the spots of blood had shown up clearly against both green and brown fallen leaves and grass. But now, as the sun sank below the horizon, the red tones in the landscape became uniformly dark, almost black. Spots of blood, splashes of lichen, fallen leaves, all were alike. The homeward trail had vanished.

We lowered our burden to the ground and looked around. We were on the edge of a glade, very like the one where the village was built. The ground rose in gentle curves all round it. Beyond, in every direction, I knew, would be other, similar glades.

"Not good." Kristin dropped to the ground with a groan. "I'm pooped."

"We need to rest anyway. And once it's daylight, we'll be able to pick up the trail again."

"I just hope the kids don't overreact and come looking for us."

I shook my head. "Consensus, remember? They'll use their heads. We can trust them."

"Let's see if we can find somewhere a bit more sheltered close by. If there's a frost tonight, we'll be freezing by morning." Kristin ran a practised eye over the terrain. I knew she would be much cleverer than I at finding a place for the night. I had been spoiled from the first, being accepted into the community and given a bed. I found myself wondering whether Jay had deliberately set Kristin up to be rejected, so that she would learn other wilderness skills; I hoped not. I hated to think that he might be manipulating us like this. *Am I naive?*

"Over there." She pointed to a sandy bank, with a small hollow where a tree had fallen long years ago. It wasn't much of a shelter, but if the wind got up it would protect our backs, and it was dry, set high above the valley and neighbouring streams.

We huddled together for warmth, with a small fire in front of us and the sandy bank at our backs. "Let's take it in turns to keep the fire going," I suggested. "I'll take first watch. I know I won't be able to sleep."

"Fine by me." In no time Kristin made herself comfortable and closed her eyes. Soon her regular breathing told me that she was asleep.

I fed the small branches we had collected into the fire and sat staring at the bright flames. I strained my ears past the crackle of the burning wood for some alien sound, but the silence was profound.

After a while it grew lighter and the bigger moon appeared above the trees, turning the forest ghostly white and black, like an ancient movie. I looked up at it and thought, *If it were the only moon in the sky, people could live in this Other Place for a long time before suspecting that they were not on Earth.* I wondered how often the moons did appear together and at what time of night.

It should be possible for us to make a kind of calendar based on their movements, I said to myself. At the moment we had no way of telling one day from another, and divisions into the weeks and months of Earth's calendar were of course meaningless. I promised myself that once we got safely home, this would be my personal priority. All civilized people develop some kind of system by which to tell the time of year.

It would be nice to have some way of reckoning the time of day too, since our Earth watches were useless. But much more important, I realized, was the ability to predict the different seasons—the appearance of grasses, the first berries, the ripening of the nuts, the onset of winter.

We'll need writing materials, I thought, *to keep a kind of almanac of our new home.* A smooth pale-coloured bark would be best, and perhaps I could develop a permanent ink by boiling twigs or leaves. I would have to experiment.

Another thing we had never considered, since our nights were normally spent safely asleep, was a map of the night sky in different seasons of the year. Right then, looking up through the trees, I could see several distinct constellations. How bright and clear the stars were! I had never imagined they could be so bright. *If only I knew where in this sky different stars appeared, we would not be lost right now.* Like a compass they would point the way home.

By then I was wide awake, excited by the possibilities of our new home, where every day we might search for meaning and order in the mysteries around us. How different from Earth, where everything important was already known! *In our whole lives here,* I thought suddenly, *we need never be bored.*

Some time later the smaller moon appeared over to my left, and I remembered how paralyzed with fear I had become when I first saw the two moons together and realized what they signified. Now, for the first time, watching those alien moons shine down upon us, I began to understand what terror Kristin must have felt, alone and rejected, with no one to share this frightening discovery with. No wonder she had despaired and almost given up.

Would the youngsters be as frightened as we were when they first learned the truth? Their cheerfulness was remarkable. They never seemed homesick or out of sorts. Perhaps to them this planet was like a wilderness camp on Earth, the sort of place where only the very richest kids could go on holiday.

How can Kristin and I tell them the truth without frightening them? Perhaps in a fable. Stories and poems delighted the young ones. Now that winter was here and the days were getting shorter, there would be more time for regular storytelling before bedtime.

Once upon a time . . . I began to spin ideas in my head, thinking of the right way to tell the story of our new world.

I was so preoccupied that I never noticed the change in the weather until a sudden hiss at the heart of the fire made me look up with a start. A white flake whirled by. And then another. The stars and the two moons had vanished and the sky was now completely overcast.

At first the falling snow delighted me. How beautiful the snowflakes were in their six-sided complexity! Was it true or false that no two flakes were alike? I began to examine them closely as they fell on the sleeves and legs of my overalls. It was some time before I realized that they were falling fast enough to threaten my fire.

I quickly added more wood, hoping that the heat would win out against the melting snow, and then I looked round anxiously for something to act as a kind of weather-screen above the fire. In the end I piled up small stones on either side and balanced a flat piece of slate on top of them. It was successful, and at once the fire began to burn more brightly. In fact it was in danger of consuming all the wood we had piled beside it.

Reluctantly I shook Kristin's shoulder. She woke at once, alert, brushing the snow from her face. "You should have woken me sooner."

"It was fine. There was nothing you could have done. But now we do need more wood."

I had barely finished speaking when she hurried off and came back dragging a dead sapling behind her. We broke up its branches and fed them into the fire.

"That roof has made a kind of draught," she noticed. "Makes for a much hotter fire."

"I was wondering about a stone fireplace inside the longhouse. If it were covered, like this, the sparks wouldn't be a danger. But getting rid of the smoke would be a major problem."

"What about a hole in the roof?"

"We'd need some kind of chimney to stop rain and snow from coming in, wouldn't we? But what could we make a chimney out of that wouldn't burn? Stones would be too heavy and might fall down and hurt someone."

"Clay maybe." Kristin brightened. "I know where to find a clay bank. We could make a shape like a bottomless pot and fasten it to the roof at the highest point opposite the door." She gestured eagerly, forming the imagined chimney in her hands.

"Yes, that's it. And if we can get clay and make a chimney, we can surely learn to make pots too, can't we?"

I was still wide awake, and though Kristin suggested that I sleep until morning, I knew I was too excited. Instead we spent the rest of the night talking about possible improvements to our way of living. How careful we must all be, we reminded each other, to make sure that anything new was also good, both for the community and for the planet itself. And to make sure that the discoveries and ideas did not come only from us, but from everybody.

"No ruined environment."

"No World Government either."

"And no police."

We fell silent in a mutual memory of those grim faces, the bulky shoulders, the stun guns. "Never," I whispered with a shiver, remembering the moment back in our apartment when Gordie had crumpled to the floor. How long ago that seemed!

"Do you remember what they said at that council meeting about the World Government coming to claim this planet and exploit its natural resources?" Kristin said suddenly.

I had a sudden horrifying vision of the forests of Xanadu obliterated, its sparkling streams running thick with noxious chemicals. "We won't let them. We simply won't!" I cried.

Kristin shrugged. "There's not a lot we could do if they decided to take over. They've got the technology. And the weapons. What have we got? A bow and arrows. A dream of building a fireplace and making clay pots."

"But we mustn't let our fear of the future get in the way of our plans for *now*. We can't think about weapons instead of clay pots. Maybe they'll forget about us."

But I didn't really believe this. The Botany Bay project must have cost a fortune, and some day the money would all have to be paid back. The cost of transporting us from Earth. The domes and force fields. The underground cave filled with electronic equipment. The devices for spying on us in the habitats. I wondered if Jay had been watching us in the village, in our daily routines. There could easily be vidcams hidden among the trees, like the security cameras on street corners back home.

Big Brother is watching you. The phrase jumped into my mind, something Dad and his friends on the Netpaper used to say. It was a quotation from some ancient book—banned of course, but a book that was almost like a bible to the dissidents.

"We mustn't ever let the others know about the World Council meeting—about the underground room. No one." Kristin's voice was hard.

"Not even Bryan and Kate and Tomas?"

151

"Uh-uh. It's our secret."

And our burden, I thought.

We sat in silence, feeding the fire. Its flames licked the slate roof and its heart glowed warmly. But the threat of the World Government hanging over us made me cold all the way through, and I shivered and wondered if I would ever be really warm again.

The flakes stopped falling shortly before dawn. A light wind got up and blew the snow from the trees and the clouds out of the sky. Slowly colour came back to the world around us. It was time to take up the burden of the beast we had come so far to slaughter and find our way home. We got to our feet, stretched our cold, cramped arms and legs and shook the snow from our clothing.

I suppose our minds had been so crowded with the million ideas, dreams and fears of our future that we had overlooked one important and obvious fact. The blood spots that we needed to lead us back to where we had waited for our prey—those precious red signs— now lay under a coating of snow.

CHAPTER TEN

It had been a light snowfall, no more than a centimetre, but it was enough to obliterate the way home.

"We've got to do something. The kids'll be worrying where we are."

"Don't panic, Ally." Kristin's dry voice made me pull myself together. "They were doing just fine before you came on the scene."

"Okay, okay. So what *should* we do?"

"Think. When we were waiting for the beasts, down by the little bay, where was the sun?"

I closed my eyes and remembered. Bars of light and shade, sun and tree shadow, patterning the little beach and the hides of the animals. "It was behind us, a bit to the left."

"Good. Then we crossed the river and headed . . ."

"Sort of westerly, I guess. But with a lot of zigzagging."

"We can't do anything about that, but it's early morning now. And the sun's over that way." She pointed.

"So if we head east, we should get back to approximately where we started." I got to my feet. The beast I had killed was lightly covered with snow, and as I brushed the powdering off its dark fur, I could feel its stiffness, its deadness. We hoisted it between us and set off without talking.

It was a magical morning, very quiet, with not even the rustle of dried leaves under our feet, just the soft carpet of snow patterned with our footprints as we

153

walked. It glistened and melted from the tops of tree branches, so that they seemed to be decorated with a million rainbow-coloured drops.

I found myself thinking of Xanadu again, and I told myself that surely, in such a perfect place, nothing could go wrong, that we would simply walk until we found ourselves back in the village with our prize, to the wonder and delight of the young ones.

"We should be bearing left," Kristin said suddenly.

"But the sun's still straight ahead."

"And moving, remember? East is a bit to the left."

Well, I know that, I told myself irritably. But I hadn't thought of it. When it came to direction-finding, Kristin was far more competent than I.

"How come you have such a good sense of which way to go?"

She gave a short laugh. "I was on my own for a long time. I had to learn that if I wanted to find my way back to my tree-home, I had better pay attention. No street signs out here."

We walked on in silence, our feet first chilled, then numbed with cold, the weight on our shoulders growing heavier pace by pace. It was an awkward load. On the way out, following the trail of blood spots, we had pushed our way through bushes, scrambled up and down the banks of streams and over hillocks. Now, with our burden, we had to go around obstacles that would not have bothered us before. Not only were we taking much longer, but there was always the chance of losing the straight line east that we were trying to follow.

"I can hear a stream," I said suddenly.

We stopped and listened intently. It was over to our right, down a slope dotted with incense trees.

"I don't remember those trees." Kristin frowned.

"The problem is, we weren't really paying attention back then."

We found the stream, cutting its way through turf and almost hidden by the grasses at its verge. Without discussion we lowered the beast and drank from the icy water. I splashed my face and gasped at the coldness.

Kristin shook her head. "Something's wrong."

"What?"

"Remember splashing through the river after the beast? The water was really warm. This is freezing."

"But it snowed last night."

"Not enough to make such a difference. No, this stream comes from some other source."

"So we really are lost?" I couldn't keep the panic out of my voice.

Kristin laughed. "We were lost before. This just confirms it." She got to her feet. "Come on. Let's go."

"Where?"

"Same plan. Head east. If we attempt to do anything else we'll end up walking in circles. Sooner or later we're bound to come on something familiar."

We changed places so that she was in the lead and all I had to do was plod along in her footsteps, keeping an even pace so that the pole did not drag on our shoulders. In this position I was staring right at the dead beast. Its head hung back so that its single horn almost touched the ground.

I suppose we should call it a unicorn, I thought idly, *though it is nothing like the mythic Earth animal*. Instead of silvery white, its coat was so dark as to be almost black, and the horn, far from being an elegant spiral of ivory and gold, was coarse and dark brown, except at its tip where it was paler and smooth—almost polished. I wondered if the horn was only an ornament or was used for digging roots.

With a handle attached it would make a useful digging tool for the community, I found myself thinking practically. As for the coat, if we could find a way of preserving the hide so it didn't harden or get smelly, it could make a small blanket or even a waterproof jacket. We had already found that the inner bark of some trees could serve as fabric, but leather and fur would be warmer and wear better.

In planning the unicorn's future use, I managed to forget for a moment that I alone was responsible for ending its life. *To be a meat-eater is a big responsibility*, I told myself, *no doubt about it.* Perhaps, if the original community had been started in an area of grassland, Jay might have introduced an intensive agriculture—some staples like beans and rice or corn. But we were in a forest, and a vegetarian diet was a luxury we could not afford. The amount of flatbread obtained from grinding grass grains only made an addition to our diet and could never be the main course . . .

I was brought up short as the pole jolted my shoulder. "Ow!"

"Sorry. Look, there in the snow. Footprints."

"Ours? Have we been going in circles after all?" I dropped my end of the pole and ran forward to look at where Kristin was pointing.

They were printed clearly in the snow. Running from left to right they led down a gentle slope. Not bare toes, but a man's shoes. *Jay's.*

"Now we'll be all right." Kristin's voice had a sudden lift to it, and I realized that she too had been afraid that we might be lost forever, that we might wander under these majestic trees until we died.

I picked up my end of the pole with a light heart and we set out again at a brisk pace. It was noon before the last of the footprints we were following melted in the sun and our feet began, painfully, to warm up.

"Isn't that the trail from the village to Jay's place?"

"I think it is. And—oh, look!"

Past her shoulder I could see, through the thinning trees, a big rock. And sitting cross-legged on the rock, his blue and black ribbons fluttering in the breeze, was Jay.

We galloped the last few metres, the unicorn swaying from side to side. "I'm so glad to see you again," I gasped.

"You did very well." He nodded approval. "To follow the wounded beast was most responsible. You'll do all right now."

"How do you know what we did? Were you watching us all the time?" I was suddenly furious. *Big Brother is watching you.*

He shrugged it off, ignoring the tone of my voice. "I had to make sure you didn't get into serious trouble."

As if we're kids, I thought and stuck my chin up. "We won't get lost again," I said confidently. "We're going to make maps. And have an almanac with star positions and the times and phases of the moons."

He looked very pleased, and in spite of myself I glowed in the warmth of his approval. Kristin said nothing, but looked off into the trees, frowning.

Jay got to his feet. "You'd better be on your way. There's a beast to skin and roast. And the children will be anxious."

"Aren't you coming with us? Won't you at least help us with the butchering?"

He shook his head. "You learned to track and hunt on your own. You've got sharp knives. You can skin a beast. Remember, back on Earth the Stone Age people used flint knives—and they were butchering mammoth!"

"Don't go. There are a million questions . . ."

"I know. And I have things I must tell you as well. But not now. I'll meet you here in two days." He strode off uphill, leaving us to carry our burden of meat back to the village, successful hunters at last.

Two days later Jay was waiting for us at the same place.

"I still don't trust him," Kristin had said.

"But you will come, won't you?"

"I'd better. You're so naive, Ally."

I could feel tears sting my eyes when she came out with that old phrase that belonged to our life on Earth. "Not really. Not any more," I muttered, and she gave me a friendly punch on the arm.

But it was hard not to be naive and believe Jay when he smiled at us, his eyes twinkling. "I have a story to tell you," he said. "And something to show you. Afterwards, questions. Let's walk along as I talk." He set off along the trail.

"The children call me Jay," he went on, "but my full name is John Jamieson. I am a psychologist, and I have spent most of my professional life working at a university which—I found out later—has close financial ties to the World Government. I was always somewhat of an idealist, and working for the World Government, especially when the police were involved, was not what I

158

had in mind. But instead of resigning and facing an uncertain future, I began to hope that I could change the minds of my superiors, induce them to understand that in intellectual freedom there was growth—"

Kristin interrupted him with one of her abrupt laughs. "I'll bet they didn't go for that."

"You're right. My boss was an advisor to WOGPO in an experiment that would have eventually led to a massive forced migration to other planets. It was a scheme to rid Earth of everyone the police wanted out of the way: artists, writers, free-thinkers of all kinds."

I opened my mouth to say, "But we know all that," and realized in time that Jay didn't know we'd broken into his computer files. "You mean people like Dad and Mom," I said instead.

"Exactly. Once released, these people were to build facilities that could be used in the exploitation of the planet's natural resources, and were to become an ongoing source of slave labour."

"Why would they go along with it? Surely they'd just rebel?"

He shook his head. "They'd be dependent on the system for food, shelter and security, wouldn't they? An initial period of forced isolation and a course of drug therapy would make them sufficiently docile."

I remembered Dad's compulsive writing, Mom's meaningless murals. The lack of care for Gordie and myself. I could feel the anger boil up inside me. "And you are in charge of all this?" I exploded. "So why are you telling us? Are you *proud* of it?"

"Hey, don't prejudge me," he said mildly. "Sure, I developed the Botany Bay project and sold the idea to my boss and ultimately to the World Government, and

I was appointed supervisor. But my real agenda was one I did *not* share with WOG. My plan was to release the children, to give them the opportunity to live in freedom, without restrictions, to become autonomous and fearless. In each child's mind I planted the idea of a perfect place—"

"Xanadu," I interrupted.

"Exactly. Through the board games in the habitats I'd already given them a subconscious blueprint for a society based on cooperation and consensus. At first they needed some physical help—how to obtain food and build shelters, for instance. But long before either of you girls came on the scene my presence was becoming less and less necessary."

A kind of unease was beginning to creep over me. Jay's explanation was beginning to sound like a farewell speech. I was still angry with him, but—

"But you're not—"

He put up a hand to stop me. "You mustn't worry about your parents and what will become of them. That has all been taken care of. My plan is to allow the force fields around each habitat to decay slowly. One day the prisoners will find that they are prisoners no longer, that they are truly free to go. It won't happen all at once. First one couple and then another will be released. And it will be up to your community of children to look after them, to help them find their feet."

"Won't it be the other way round?" Kristin gave a humourless laugh. "With them bossing us? Telling us how to run our lives?"

Jay shook his head. "They have already been so brainwashed by the degraded quality of life on Earth that they must forget and then learn how to start over again.

You will find they have no memory of where they have come from or what they did back on Earth. They will need help and loving care to adjust to this new world. Don't worry—this stage isn't going to start right away, not until the summer after next. By then I am confident that you'll be so well established that you'll be able to absorb them into your community without difficulty."

After he stopped talking we walked on in stunned silence. Even Kristin had nothing to say. We had been climbing as Jay talked, and now I realized that we were on the way back to Jay's secret cave in the mountain.

"It's . . . it's incredible," I stammered at last. "You're saying that this is really our place? For ever and ever? With no WOGPO interfering, spying on us?"

Jay smiled. "That's what I'm saying."

"It's a lie," Kristin retorted. "Don't be fooled by him, Ally. He's told us just enough of the truth to make himself look good. What he hasn't told us is what we found out by breaking his security code and reading all the details of the arrangement that WOG made. We know that sometime in the future WOG intends to send ships from Earth to take us over, to enslave us and destroy this place with their ugly technology. What kind of life can we have with *that* threat hanging over us?"

Jay stopped walking and turned to stare at us. Then he began to laugh. "Full of surprises! I certainly picked the right two! You not only track me to my headquarters and brave the stairway down the chute, but you crack my security code!" He paused. "Well, maybe it's better this way."

From the twinkle in his eye I could tell that he wasn't really disconcerted by our actions. Had he expected them? Trickster Jay—we would probably never know for sure.

He went on talking. "You're quite right. Of course WOG plans to return to this planet—oh, not next year, perhaps not even in your lifetime. But sometime, sooner or later. This is why I've brought you here today. I want you to see exactly what I'm going to do, so you can truly believe in your freedom."

By the time he'd finished talking, we had reached the ridge and it took all our concentration to climb down the gorge to the small plateau beneath the waterfall, where the river ran underground. *Through caverns measureless to man.* I remembered my favourite poem.

The thunder of the falls beat at our ears. The spray rose high and a rainbow formed magically above the place where the river vanished underground.

Jay gestured for us to stand back, and then he approached the lip of the chute, his feet only centimetres away from the slippery edge. He took something like a WOGPO stun gun from his pocket, and just for a second my heart flipped, and through my mind flashed the thought that he was going to get rid of us, that his whole story had been a ploy to lure us here, to the edge of the chute, so that he could stun us and tip our helpless bodies down into the void.

In that second when my imagination ran away with me, he lifted the weapon and pointed it at the right side of the chute. A laser beam shot out. The rock it struck glowed and melted, hissing and steaming into the falling water. Jay swept the laser up and down until there was no evidence of steps or handholds. Water filled the whole cavity, washing the debris down the chute into the unseen depths below. There was no sign that anyone had ever been in this place, that in the darkness far below was a labyrinth of passages and caves, a secret room full of WOGPO spying devices.

Jay backed away from the brink, pocketed his weapon and put his arms over our shoulders, drawing us away from the thundering water. We climbed the cliff in silence—and in total bewilderment. Once we had gained the top of the ridge again, and the noise of the falls had abated to a distant roar, he spoke again.

"The equipment you saw inside the cave is already destroyed. All connections with Earth have been severed."

He is *on our side*, I thought. But Kristin was a harder sell. "That won't stop them from coming. Maybe even sooner—to find out what went wrong."

He shook his head. "No, they won't, because I'm taking my report back to Earth. It's unfortunate, I'll tell them. I was wrong. Project Botany Bay has been a total failure. The parents and children are all dead. WOGPO won't come here, I promise you. You're safe."

"The Government'll be furious," I gasped. "They'll kill you."

He gave a wry smile. "I certainly won't get promoted, but Dr. Kereluk is powerful enough to protect me. After all, it was his decision to go ahead with the project and allow me to oversee it."

"How do you get back to Earth?" Kristin asked.

"I've a small flipper parked in orbit." He pointed up at the wintry blue sky. "I just have to transport up by SMT and set course for the nearest space station. Then I hitch a ride back to Earth and face the music." He laughed again.

How brave he is, I thought. *Laughing.* "But you *will*

come back?" There was something horribly final about this conversation.

He shook his head. "Oh no, Ally. I can't do that. You kids are on your own. The habitats will slowly shut down, as I explained. Your parents will come out. You'll care for them. And for—for Xanadu." He looked up at the clear, unpolluted sky and took a deep breath of incense-scented air. "How I shall miss Xanadu!"

"But you can't not come back," I cried. "That means we're never going to see you again. Suppose we need help?" I was thinking only of myself then. Of us. It wasn't until much later that I began to think of Jay, and of what it must have meant to him to leave the promise and hope of Xanadu for a harsh and despoiled Earth.

"I'll be off then," he said in a matter-of-fact voice. "You'll do a great job here, I know you will. I'm counting on you." He slipped a small phone-like device from his pocket, pressed a button—and vanished.

It has taken us a long time to get used to the fact that he won't be back. That we will never again see the flutter of his blue and black blue jay costume appearing from between the trees.

Perhaps it was harder for the youngsters. Because they didn't see him go, for a long time they refused to believe that he wouldn't be back. We made up a story, Kristin and I—a number of stories, in fact—that we told during the long, dark evenings of that first winter in the longhouse.

We told them how Jay planned that this world should be for children to live in, a world always to be kept beautiful and unspoiled. We reminded them of what he had taught us about cooperation and consensus. And we told them that one day soon they would be reunited with their lost parents, the much-loved fathers and mothers of us all, and that we would take care of them, as they had once taken care of us when we were little. We told them that that was what Jay had said was going to happen, that though *he* would not return, our parents would, and that in loving and caring for them, and for this Other Place, we would be doing what Jay had planned for them.

Once I had thought, jokingly, that we would never find a name for this planet that everyone would agree on. Not Xanadu, which was Gordie's dream. Nor Big Rock Candy Mountain, which was Bobbie's. Nor any of the other perfect names that had drawn the children from their prisons into this new world.

So it was a surprise to me, when the name was first suggested, that everyone agreed upon it at once without any argument at all. But of course it should really have been no surprise, for it was only right and fitting that we would call our new home *Jay's World*.

Sometimes when I am alone, looking up at the newly familiar stars, I think of Jay and of how much he gave up to ensure that we would be forever free. In the midst of city smog and the jangle of traffic, does he still remember the scent of the incense trees and the quietness of the forest? Does he look up at the night sky, as I am looking at it now, and search for the one small, insignificant star that marks our home? Does he remember us, as we will always remember him?

Thank you, Jay. Dear trickster Jay.